Justice

Born in Rugby, North Dakota, Larry Watson received his BA and
MA in English from the University of North Dakota and his Ph.D.
in creative writing from the University of Utah. He is the author
of the novel *In a Dark Time* and a chapbook of poetry, *Leaving
Dakota*, all published in the US. *Montana 1948* won the US
Milkweed National Fiction Prize and was his debut novel in the
UK. He currently teaches English at the University of Wisconsin
and lives in Stevens Point, Wisconsin.

Also by Larry Watson

In a Dark Time

Leaving Dakota

Montana 1948

Justice

LARRY WATSON

PAN BOOKS

First published 1995 by POCKET BOOKS

a division of Simon & Schuster Inc.
1230 Avenue of the Americas, New York, NY 10020

First published in Great Britain 1997 by Pan Books
an imprint of Macmillan Publishers Ltd
25 Eccleston Place, London SW1W 9NF
and Basingstoke

Associated companies throughout the world

ISBN 0 330 35018 8

1 3 5 7 9 8 6 4 2

A CIP catalogue record for this book is available from
the British Library.

Typeset by SetSystems Ltd, Saffron Walden, Essex
Printed and bound in Great Britain by
Mackays of Chatham plc, Chatham, Kent

For Susan

I would like to thank my editor, Emilie Buchwald, for her keen and intelligent eye and her thoughtful suggestions. Working with the people at Milkweed Editions has been a salutary experience. A special thanks to Arlinda, Beryl, Diane, Ellen, Fiona, Scott, and Teresa for their enthusiasm and good will.

My agent, Sharon Friedman, deserves thanks for the encouragement and friendship she has provided.

My mother, Ruth Watson, has helped keep my plains heritage alive. Her memories and her stories have offered inspiration, and, from the earliest, her love and understanding have given me confidence. I can never thank her enough.

My daughters, Elly and Amy, have enriched my life beyond measure.

My wife, Susan, first reader and best friend, provided the challenge and impetus that made these words possible. Thank you and more.

Contents

Outside the Jurisdiction
(1924)

✿ ✿ ✿

W HEN Tommy Salter, Lester Hoenig, and the Hayden brothers left Bentrock, Montana, at dawn, only a gentle snow—flakes fat as bits of white cloth—fell from the November sky. But the spaces between those flakes filled in fast, and soon it became impossible to see more than fifty yards down the highway. Where the road dipped or was sheltered from the wind, snow lay so thick on the road that the bottom of the Model T, even with its high clearance, scraped the tops of drifts.

"We get high-centered," Tommy Salter said from the backseat, "we're done for. We ain't going nowhere."

Frank Hayden, the driver, said, "We're all right." He tightened his grip on the steering wheel and kept the car aimed for the tracks made by the last car that had passed that way.

"You bring a shovel?" Lester asked.

Frank glanced quickly at his brother then shook his head.

Wesley Hayden tilted his head until it rested against the window's icy glass. He closed his eyes and concentrated on the car's slow, wobbly motion down the highway. God*damn,* he had wanted so badly for this trip to go well. Next fall, Frank, two years older than Wesley, would be in college, seven hundred miles away at the University of Minnesota. This could be the last time the brothers took this trip together for years. For years? Wesley reconsidered. This could be the last time. Ever.

"Anyone want to turn around? Go back?" Frank asked.

Tommy laughed. "Where the hell you going to turn around?"

"It could let up," Lester offered. "Down the road. I guess I'm for pushing on."

Wesley kept his eyes closed. "It isn't going to let up."

"You know that, do you?" Frank asked his brother.

"You know it too," Wesley answered.

"We ain't going to freeze to death anyway," said Tommy.

Wesley knew Tommy was referring to the three bottles of bootleg whiskey, purchased for them by Dale Paris, a hired hand on the Hayden ranch.

"What's the nearest town?" Frank asked.

Lester asked, "Are we in North Dakota?"

"We've been in North Dakota since breakfast," Tommy answered.

"You know damn well the closest town," Wesley said to his brother. "McCoy."

Frank nodded. "If it doesn't let up I'm thinking we'll head for McCoy. That's got to be less than fifty miles."

The plan had been to leave their home in northeast Montana, cross over into North Dakota, and head south. Eventually they would set up camp on the banks of the Little Missouri and from there hunt the red rocky bluffs, the dark wooded draws, and the sagebrush flats of the Dakota

Badlands. They had hunted that region for years, and just last year they returned with four deer and over fifty pheasant and partridge. Lester had even shot a coyote. Of course last year the weather had been much different—three days of sunshine and uncommonly warm temperatures.

"I don't hear you," Frank said, cupping his ear to the group.

"What's in McCoy?" asked Lester. "Anything?"

Tommy laughed. "It's right off the reservation. You know what's in McCoy."

Lester looked down the road. "It sure as hell ain't letting up."

"What about you?" Frank asked Wesley.

"Do what you want. You don't need my permission." When they were first planning this trip, Wesley had hoped that he and his brother would go alone. But Frank invited friends, and now Wesley not only had to share his brother, but since Lester and Tommy were Frank's age, Wesley was stuck being the youngest as well. He was the little brother; he didn't have any influence with this group. Hell, Wesley had hoped they'd actually hunt. Just hunt. But this snow covered that hope too.

Frank said to Wesley, "I'm not taking anyone where they don't want to go. If you don't want to go to McCoy, say the word."

"I'll camp out in the snow," Lester said. "Don't bother me."

"Go to McCoy," Wesley said to his brother. "Fuck if I care."

Frank took his hand from the steering wheel and slapped

his brother gently on the arm. "Hey—it's outside the jurisdiction, right?"

Outside the jurisdiction. How many times had Wesley heard his brother use that phrase? They were the sons of Julian Hayden, the sheriff of Mercer County, Montana, and that fact made Frank's and Wesley's lives both easier and more difficult. They grew up knowing that if they ever got into trouble, their father, proud and protective of his sons, would bail them out. Yet knowing this, they felt they had to behave so it wouldn't seem as though they were taking advantage of their father's position. Only when they got out of town, out of the county, out of the jurisdiction, did they feel as though they could be other than the sons of Julian Hayden.

"Where we going to stay?" Lester asked. "I don't mind sleeping in the car if we can find someplace to park it out of the wind. Shit, I'll sleep in the tent for that matter."

"We'll get a room at the hotel," said Frank.

"They got a hotel?" asked Lester.

"Hotel or a boardinghouse. I forget which."

"It's a hotel," Tommy said. "I think."

"You think they'll give us a room?" Lester asked.

"Hell, yes," Frank replied. "Why not? If we can pay they'll give us a room."

Wesley understood that Lester's true concern was over money. A good many families in Mercer County were poor, but the Hoenigs were worse off than most. Their family was large (Wesley could never keep track—were there nine or ten kids?), and whether it was the land it sat on or Mr. Hoenig's incompetence Wesley never knew for sure, but their farm, year in and year out, was one of the least productive in the area. Lester tried to cover their poverty by pretending not to care about what other boys cared about—new shotguns or rifles, cars, horses, pretty girls, baseball gloves. Frank and Wesley's mother had stopped giving Frank's hand-me-downs to Wesley; instead she had Frank give them to the shorter, slighter Lester.

"Me and Frank will pay for the room," Wesley offered.

"You sure?" Lester said.

Frank picked up on his brother's suggestion. "The trip's our idea. Hell, McCoy's my idea. It's only fair."

"Okay by me," agreed Tommy.

"I still wonder if they'll give us a room," worried Lester.

"Frank's right," Tommy said. "If we got the money, we're in. That's McCoy."

Frank shook his head. "Pop says it's not as wide open as it used to be."

"That's not what you said last summer," Tommy replied.

"What?" Lester asked. "What about last summer?"

"We had a baseball tournament over there," Tommy said.

Wesley interrupted. "It's hardly even cattle country around there now. Fucking wheat farmers."

"Where were you?" Frank asked Lester. "How come you didn't play?"

"Working," Lester answered. "We was bringing in a crop of hay. Trying to. What there was." He turned back to Tommy. "What happened in McCoy?"

Tommy leaned toward Frank. "You want me to tell him?"

Frank shrugged.

"How long has it been since we saw another car?" Wesley asked.

"You never see anybody on this road," Frank said. "Even when the weather's good."

"You wonder why they put the money in a road nobody uses," Wesley said.

Tommy tapped his fingers over his mouth in an imitation war chant. "Woo-woo-woo-woo! You didn't hear? Frank got himself a little Indian gal in McCoy last summer. Got her good."

Tommy had stolen a box of cigars from Douglas's Rexall before they left, and he and Lester had been smoking since they drove out of town. The car was drafty, but cigar smoke still gathered so thickly in the backseat that when Wesley turned around it looked as though Tommy and Lester sat in their own little blizzard. Ahead or behind, Wesley thought, you can't see a goddamn thing.

Lester leaned toward Frank. "Did you force her? Did you have to force her?"

Frank's laugh sounded like a bark in the car's close quarters. "Where did you get an idea like that? Force her. Such language. You read that somewhere?"

Tommy was laughing too. "Shit, she followed him around with her skirt over her head practically. She let him fuck her right by the ball field. In somebody's truck, wasn't it?"

"How come I never heard about this?" asked Lester.

Wesley wiped his nose on the back of his glove. "You should've. Seemed like everybody in the whole school knew about it."

"Even Loretta?" asked Lester. Loretta was Loretta Gerber, the girl with whom Frank was supposed to be going steady.

Frank's laughter stopped. "She better not. If Loretta found out, I'd know someone was telling tales out of school. Someone would get his ass whipped."

"Hey, she ain't going to hear anything from me," said Tommy. "But it's hard to keep a secret in Bentrock."

Frank's smile returned. "I don't know about that."

Wesley turned away from his brother and waited. He thought he knew what would come next.

Frank said, "You haven't got the facts quite right."

Wesley recognized those words as the same ones that came often from their father's mouth. When asked about a crime in the county, their father loved to let people speculate on the incident and then to correct them, smiling slyly, with the phrase, "You haven't got the facts quite right."

"I'm surprised at you, Tommy," said Frank. "What with you being there and all. I didn't fuck that little Indian girl."

"The hell."

"I'm telling you."

Lester punched Tommy in the shoulder. "Now who's telling stories."

Tommy cocked his fist but didn't deliver a blow. "Goddamn it!"

"That's right," said Frank. "I didn't just fuck that little squaw. . . . I fucked her mama too."

Tommy fell back laughing. He kicked the back of the seat so hard Wesley could feel Tommy's boots right through the springs and the horsehair.

"No shit?" said Lester. "The both of them? How did you. . . . Did you do 'em at the same time?"

"At the same time, Lester? Fellow would have to have two peckers to do that. Besides, no mama and her daughter are that close."

"What did the old one look like?" Tommy wanted to know.

"She wasn't *old*. She was actually pretty young to have a daughter that age." Frank took one hand off the steering wheel and rested it on the gearshift. "She wasn't bad looking. But she was on the plump side. Like squaws can get."

"Jesus," said Tommy. "The both of them."

"It wasn't easy. Cost me three bottles of Ole Norgaard's homemade wine. One for the daugher, two for her mama."

When Wesley heard that he remembered a day the previous summer when he and his brother had ridden with their mother out to Ole Norgaard's place, a little tarpaper shack just outside Bentrock. Ole, everyone agreed, had a gift for growing fruits and vegetables, and even people who had their own gardens bought produce from Ole. He also made homemade beer and wine, and a good many men in the county swore on the superiority of Ole's products. Once Prohibition went into effect, their father made no effort to close down Ole. Furthermore, if any local man wanted to make a little home brew or buy a couple bottles of gin when he was in Minneapolis and bring it home with him, the sheriff would not object. However, if an outsider tried to come into the county and operate a still or if someone began to run large quantities of bootleg whiskey down from Canada, the sheriff would stop that in a minute. He did not object to a man taking a drink—

he was as fond of Ole Norgaard's beer as anyone—but he would not tolerate an outsider making a profit on the county's residents.

On that day, Frank and Wesley waited by the car while their mother went out to Ole's garden with him. Ole allowed his best customers—and certainly Mrs. Hayden qualified—to pick out their vegetables while they were still on the vine or the stalk or in the ground. Mrs. Hayden had come for sweet corn, and Ole would find a dozen of the best ears for her.

Once they were certain they weren't being watched, Frank and Wesley went inside Ole's shack. The interior was dim, musty, and cluttered with piles of yellowing Swedish newspapers, rows of ripening vegetables, and stacks of wooden crates. The boys knew exactly what they were looking for and found it quickly—the case of bottles of dandelion wine, their corks covered with sealing wax. Frank and Wesley each took two bottles—they had agreed that taking more would somehow escalate their crime into something that would deserve severe punishment if they were caught.

Weeks passed and no occasion arose that Wesley considered fitting to bring out his bottles of wine. Then the baseball team—of which his brother was the star—went to McCoy, North Dakota, to play in a tournament. While the team was gone, Wesley, on a hunch, checked his cache to see if the bottles were still there. They were gone. Now he knew what his brother had done with the wine.

Wesley Hayden had never even kissed a girl, unless you counted the quick little brush on the lips Esther Radner gave him at a skating party last winter. And Wesley discounted that incident, since Esther had kissed virtually every male at the party as part of an experiment she said she was conducting to see whose lips were coldest. Wesley was shy around girls, and in their presence being tongue-tied sometimes translated into what looked like anger. On more than one occasion a boy or girl came to him saying something like "Rebecca wants to know why you're mad at her." Ironically, Rebecca was probably the last person in the world he was mad at—why, he was as likely to be in love with her! Yet somehow in his ineptitude he would communicate exactly the opposite message.

Part of the problem was that he couldn't decide what he wanted girls for. It could change within a day, an hour, a minute. One instant he could regard them as helpless creatures who needed his strength and protection. Around them you had to put on your best manners, your most chivalrous attitude. When he thought of girls in this way he wanted only to be with them, to walk down the streets of Bentrock with one of the pretty girls from his school on his arm. Yet in the next second he might think of performing the most obscene, degrading act with this very girl—she would have no more humanity or identity than the hand with which he masturbated daily.

That was why he was so angry to hear Frank's story of the two Indians in McCoy. Damn it, Wesley thought, the wine was his, so the Indian girl should have been as well. The situation was perfect for him. He would have been in a strange community where he knew no one, and no one knew him. He could not have damaged his reputation there, because he had none. And he would not have to worry about facing the girl again.

But in his heart Wesley knew he was deceiving himself. The wine may have been Wesley's, but the audacity to barter it for sex was Frank's. In fact, the incident illustrated perfectly the difference between the brothers. Frank had put that stolen wine to use; Wesely could not think of a reason to take his bottles out of hiding. Wesley hated and loved his brother for being everything that Wesley could never be.

"So let's not be too quick to get into that hooch," Frank announced to the group. "You never know what we might be able to buy with it."

"We ain't going to get a taste?" Lester asked.

Tommy punched Lester again on the arm. "What would you rather have—a piece of ass or a drink of whiskey?"

Wesley turned around in time to see Lester hang his tongue from his mouth.

Tommy took his cigar from his mouth and said quietly to the Hayden brothers, "You know, I don't care anymore if I don't get off a shot this weekend. This is turning into my kind of hunting trip."

Tommy fell back against the backseat, and Frank looked over at his brother and rolled his eyes toward the roof of the car. Wesley pretended not to see his brother's gesture and turned quickly to the window.

Was the snow letting up? Wesley had been gauging its intensity all day by looking at the snow against a dark background, an occasional tree trunk or telephone pole or fence post, and as the snow came down harder it became harder to see any sharp, dark outlines. But now his vision seemed to clear slightly. Maybe the snow would stop or let up enough to let them spend these days as they had originally planned.

In his bedroom, tucked into the frame of his mirror, Wesley had a photograph taken on this trip two years earlier: Wesley, Frank, their father, Len McAuley, their father's deputy, and Arnold Spence, a friend of their father's, are standing in front of the camp tent. They are dressed in hunting gear, and since they have been gone for a few days their clothes are rumpled and dirty. The adults have three days' growth of beard. They are all holding rifles in their gloved hands, and they are smiling widely. They are standing next to four freshly killed deer. The deer—two of them with impressive racks of antlers—are strung up from a tree limb. Their heads are tilted to the sky at such strange angles it looks as though they have been hanged to death. A dusting of snow covers the ground, and you can tell by the expressions on the men's faces—their smiles are tight, their noses and cheeks are a darker gray in the photograph—that the day is cold. You can also tell that not a single one of them would rather be anywhere else in the world. Wesley had hoped that he would be able to take a similar photograph to commemorate this trip. He doubted now if he would even unpack his gun, much less his camera.

They drove into McCoy in early afternoon. The snow had subsided, but, as if to support their decision to stop, the wind had increased, clearing the highway of snow in one place and then piling it high with drifts in another. As the snow whipped across the road, the asphalt itself appeared and disappeared under those rolling, waving, ghostly snakes.

They parked in front of the Overland Hotel, a square two-story building of unevenly laid reddish orange brick. Two rows of windows, unnaturally small for the building's size, stared down at the snowy street.

The old woman at the desk regarded the boys suspiciously when they came in. She was short and squat and had tiny dark eyes. The blanket she kept wrapped around her shoulders like a shawl dragged on the floor as she moved around behind the desk. She gave them the key to a room but warned them, "You boys. I got other guests. Make trouble and you go." Her accent was thick, Germanic.

Frank asked her, "Where should we put the car?"

"Where you got it now?"

"Out in front."

"What's the matter with there?"

Their second-floor room had a bed with an iron bedstead, a dresser with a porcelain pitcher and washbowl, a straight-backed chair, and a small table beside the bed. Over the bed hung a small framed picture of the Last Supper that looked as though it had been cut from a magazine. The window shade was up and the lace curtains tied back, but the window looked out on nothing but a snowy field.

Lester lifted the hem of the chenille bedspread and peered under the bed. "Is there a slop bucket or somethin'? As long as there isn't a biffy."

Wesley recalled that Lester's family did not have indoor plumbing.

"Bathroom's down the hall," Frank said.

Tommy pointed at Lester and laughed. "You never stayed in a hotel before, have you?"

"What the hell for?" Lester answered angrily. With his boot he shoved his canvas duffle against the wall. "Don't bother me to sleep outside. I'll do it tonight if you like."

"Nobody has to sleep outside," said Frank. "But we do have to set up a plan."

Tommy bounced up and down on the edge of the bed, making the springs whine. "What kind of plan?"

"Let's say one of us wants to bring a guest up here," Frank explained. "The others are going to have to clear out for a spell."

"A guest?" asked Lester.

Wesley felt sorry for Lester. He stood in the middle of the room, still wearing his coat with the dirty matted sheepskin lining and with the earflaps on his fraying wool cap tied down. Lester was the most skilled outdoorsman of the group, a crack shot with a rifle and a shotgun and a fisherman who could land a cast within inches of a lily pad. If they brought down a deer Lester would be invaluable; he could field dress a deer with a speed and efficiency that a butcher might envy. Yet if a tree were growing up through the floor of the hotel room it would not look more out of place in these surroundings than Lester.

Tommy stopped bouncing on the bed. He looked up at Lester. "You know, you're so fucking dumb sometimes it hurts. You know that—it *hurts*."

Lester looked to Frank like a dog appealing to its master.

"If one of us gets a girl," Frank said slowly, "we've got to have a plan so he can have the room to himself."

"If he wants to keep her to himself," said Tommy.

Lester snorted. "You ain't too cocky, are you. Where the hell you going to find you a girl?"

Tommy started bouncing on the bed again. "You know her name, don't you," he said to Frank. "Goddamn. You know her name!"

Frank shrugged his shoulders. "I remember her first name. That's all."

With a bound Tommy was off the bed and at Frank's side. "Come on. Get her over here. Her and her mama both. We'll have us some red meat for supper."

Frank shoved Tommy aside. "You wouldn't know what to do with it."

Tommy put his head and shoulders down like a football lineman and pretended to run into Frank. He stopped his charge short and came up grinning. "You try me. Get her up here. Try me."

"Get your own."

Lester was searching through the pile of duffels and packs. "Where's those fucking cigars." He came up with one in his mouth. "You're going to look for girls. Don't make me laugh. You ain't going to find any. In the meantime we ain't supposed to get into that liquor. Shit. We'll end up taking it back home. Three days and I won't get off a shot or pull a cork. *Shit*."

27

Wesley suddenly felt ill. After those long hours in the cold car the hotel's warmth was too much for him. There didn't seem to be enough air, and he couldn't take a deep breath because of the strong smell of camphor in the room. He tried moving away from the chest of drawers but the odor followed him. He knew he wouldn't be able to take the smell of Lester's cigar.

"I'm going down to the lobby," he announced.

"What for?" asked Frank.

"Not for anything. I'm just going down there."

"Suit yourself."

As he left the room, Wesley heard Lester say with disgust, "You want 'em, you go get 'em."

Wesley sat in the lobby on a hard, oil-stained horsehair sofa. There were smells here too—cigar smoke again and something like creosote. He kept himself turned to the side so he could look out the window and monitor the storm. He was certain now; yes, the snow had stopped falling, but the wind continued to rise and as much snow filled the air from the ground up as it had earlier from the sky down. He didn't know why he still cared. He knew he wasn't going hunting. There was nothing to do but wait out the hours and days until it was time to return to Montana. Maybe they'd go back tomorrow. Tonight they'd look for girls, find none, get drunk, and drive home early tomorrow. The hotel had presented them with an expense none of them had planned on.

While Wesley stared out the window the old woman from behind the desk approached him. She walked slowly, taking tiny steps and listing from side to side. She stood in front of Wesley a long time before she spoke.

"Where's your family?"

The question was simple, yet Wesley had trouble understanding what she meant. Did she want to know how near his family was, if he had relatives around McCoy?

"My brother's upstairs."

She twisted her mouth as though she were trying to dislodge something from her teeth.

"You got more than a brother, don't you."

"In Bentrock, Montana. Like we wrote on the register."

She snorted. "If I could read that I could read it for myself."

"It's in Montana." Wesley realized he had already said that, and he began to explain where in Montana. "Northeast Montana. Not far from the Canadian border. Bentrock is the county seat." His voice softened and trailed off until, like snow falling, it was barely there. "My—I mean, our—parents live there." The old woman turned and walked away, but Wesley could not stop. "We go on this hunting trip every year, but this is the first year none of our folks came along. My brother's going to be in college next year. He's got offers from all over. . . ."

The day had gotten colder, but the boys walked down the wooden walkway of McCoy's main street with their coats flapping open in the wind. They had brought along knit caps and wool caps with earflaps, but now all of them but Lester had switched to Stetsons. They wore them pulled down low and held onto them to keep them from blowing off. They walked four abreast but no one had to step aside for them because no one else was on the street. They were going to the Buffalo Cafe, an eatery the woman at the hotel recommended. The cafe was, she said, "where most of the guests eat. Families too."

As they entered the cafe, a bell attached to the door announced their arrival, but no one came forth to greet them. They stamped the snow from their boots, brushed flakes from their sleeves, and slapped their hats on their trousers.

The skin under Lester's nose was raw from his jacket's rough wool, but he wiped his nose one more time on his sleeve. "And you were going to find you some girls. Hell, there's nobody out today. We ain't even going to get a hot meal."

"They're open," said Frank. "The door wasn't locked."

The cafe reminded Wesley of someone's home. The walls were covered with peeling, yellowing wallpaper, the windows with lace curtains, the floor with mismatched rag rugs. If it weren't for the fact that there were four oilcloth-covered tables instead of one, Wesley believed he could have been in the dining room of a neighbor back in Bentrock. Then he noticed two more differences hanging on the walls: a blackboard listing the day's menu and the prices, and, in place of a family photograph, a massive buffalo head, horned and glossy-eyed, its shaggy, matted fur the darkest presence in this brightly lit room.

Tommy pretended to sight a rifle at the buffalo and then squeezed the imaginary trigger. Deep in his throat he imitated the muffled sound of a gunshot and then rocked back on his heels as if the gun had a tremendous recoil.

At that moment a tall, gray-haired woman came through a curtained doorway and into the cafe's bright interior. She wore a man's faded plaid flannel shirt over her print dress. The sleeves of the shirt were rolled to the elbow revealing her muscular forearms. She was wiping her hands on a dish towel.

Two Indian girls, teenagers, came out of the back room behind the tall woman. When Wesley saw the girls he almost gasped out loud. Jesus, there they were. Frank and Tommy wanted girls and there they were. The sons of bitches didn't even have to go looking for them.

One of the girls was almost as tall as the gray-haired woman, while the other girl was short and overweight. The shorter girl had a pretty face though, and something about the way she never stopped smiling made Wesley think she was a friendly, good-natured person who would be easy to talk to. Her black hair hung loose, past her shoulders. Under her un-buttoned wool coat she wore a dark blue dress with a small white collar. Her black rubber overshoes were too big for her; she had to slide her feet to keep the boots from slipping off. With every step she took, the overshoe buckles jingled and the wet rubber squeaked on the wooden floor.

But of the two, the taller girl was the real beauty. She was slender and graceful and carried herself confidently. Her hair was plaited in two long braids that hung down her chest. She wore an unbuttoned coat and dress identical to the other girl's, but on her feet instead of galoshes were high buckskin leggings that whispered across the floor when she walked. Then, as she came closer, Wesley saw the scar. It was a pale diagonal seam that extended from near her nose to her upper lip, and whatever had happened to her must have cut through muscle because her lip curled up slightly.

Because of her stern expression and the haughty look her curled lip gave her, Wesley felt that he and this Indian girl were somehow similar, both slightly disapproving of the company they were in, both present and yet not present in every room they entered. Then Wesley caught himself. This was just an Indian girl; he had no good reason to think she was anything like what he imagined.

The gray-haired woman spoke over her shoulder to the girls. "Your ride doesn't come, that's it. You're out of luck. That's a private phone."

The short girl kept smiling. "We know. Thank you."

The woman saw the four boys standing by the door. "You here to eat? Or just come in out of the snow?"

Frank spoke for them. "We'd like to get something to eat. If it's no bother."

"Oh, it's a bother all right. That's why I make people pay me."

Tommy was the only one who laughed.

"But you got to sit down, boys. That's the way it works. You sit down and I bring the food to you on a plate."

Lester began to walk toward the back of the cafe, but Frank caught him by the hem of the coat. "Over here."

32

They hesitated like a flock of birds that take an instant to understand the direction they're heading, then turned and followed Frank to a table by the window. The girls were already seated at an adjoining table.

As soon as they sat down, Tommy began to talk to the girls. "You gals need a ride somewheres? Is that what I heard?"

The tall girl stared out at the blowing snow, but the plump girl looked over at the four boys.

"How about it?" Tommy asked again. "We got a car. We can take you."

"Someone's coming for us," the shorter girl answered.

Tommy ignored her reply. "Out to the reservation? Is that where you're going?"

The tall girl cast a withering look their way. "We go to Sacred Heart."

The other girl nodded. "We live here in town."

"Sacred Heart," Frank said in a voice so soft Wesley barely recognized it as his brother's. "The high school, right?"

The plump girl kept smiling that smile that never seemed to increase or decrease in its intensity. "We're seniors," she said.

"We are too," Frank replied. "Well, three of us. My brother's a sophomore."

Wesley winced. At least Frank hadn't said which one was his brother.

Tommy leaned over the table. "Where do you want a ride to?"

Frank waved his hand over the oilcloth, a small, quick gesture that looked as if he might have been brushing crumbs away, but Wesley knew what his brother was doing: Frank was trying to tell Tommy to shut up, to tell all of them that they should allow him to do the talking.

"We're sort of stuck here," Frank said to the girls. "We were heading down toward the Badlands to do some hunting. When it started snowing and blowing we decided we better get into town and hunker down. We're staying at the Overland Hotel."

"Where did you come from?" the shorter girl asked.

"We come a ways," said Frank. "We're from Montana. From Bentrock. You know where that is?"

Wesley thought he heard the tall girl sniff derisively at Frank's question.

The other girl giggled. "Montana. My uncle says Montana's nothing but cows and cowboys."

Frank smiled at her. "He's not too far off. It's the Wild West, that's for sure."

Tommy almost came out of his chair. "Yeah? You know what we call North Dakotans?"

"I'll tell you one thing," Lester put in. "There ain't a restaurant in the whole damn state of Montana where you have to wait this long to get waited on."

Frank changed the subject. "How's the food here? She's not going to try to poison us, is she? Just because we're from Montana."

Without looking in their direction the tall girl said something that sounded to Wesley like "Ah-nish-ah-pahn-ta," and her friend laughed.

"What the hell was that about?" Lester asked.

"She said——" she had to wait until her laughter subsided—— "she said it's good enough for cowboys."

"What was that?" Frank asked. "Sioux?"

The tall girl turned their way once more. *"Lakota,"* she said sharply.

Lester asked, "Is she ever going to take our order?"

Frank slid his chair over to the girls' table. "Say something else," he said. "In Lakota, I mean. I like the way it sounds."

Wesley was amazed. He couldn't believe how gentle, how soft-spoken his brother was. He had seen Frank around girls before, at school, at football games, at the drugstore counter, and Frank was always louder and funnier and bigger and bolder than anyone else. Girls couldn't stay away from him— because he was handsome, yes, but also because there was something dangerous about him. They had to keep an eye on him. And they were right. Wesley had heard the way his brother talked about girls, as if he could tear chunks from them, get "a piece of ass," "a little tail," "some tit," or how he could punish them with sex, make them "moan" or "squeal" or "beg for more," or how he'd reduce them to animality and have them "crawling on their hands and knees." Now Wesley saw this courtly young gentleman who seemed more inter-ested in the Indian language than . . . than what Wesley knew his brother wanted from these girls.

The girl did say something else in Lakota, another phrase that sounded to Wesley like a little run of soft sighs punctu-ated with sudden stops of consonants. She did not speak to Frank, however. She addressed her friend.

"What is it? What did she say?" asked Frank.

The plump girl scowled. "Not for you, she said. We don't speak our tongue for you to listen."

Lester pointed to his companions. "Do you know what you want to eat? Should I just go back there and tell her what we want? Me, I'm going to have a fried ham sandwich. Maybe some soup." He leaned toward the plump girl. "Hey. How about that tomato soup. Is it the kind made with milk?"

She looked at Lester as if he were the one speaking a foreign tongue.

Tommy nudged Frank's chair with the toe of his boot. "You going to ask 'em?"

Frank ignored him. "I wasn't making fun of your language. Really. I just like to hear you talk it."

Tommy kicked Frank's chair again. "Tell them about the whiskey."

"What's he talking about?" the plump girl asked.

Frank gave Tommy a dark look and mouthed the words "shut up."

"What?" she asked again.

"My partner here was hoping—I mean, we were all hoping—since our hunting trip is all fouled up we were hoping you could cheer us up."

The plump girl turned to her friend with an expression that seemed to Wesley to be beseeching. She wanted to, Wesley knew, but her friend wouldn't have anything to do with them.

"I was going to ask you to show us around town," Frank said. "But I better not. You're just too damn unfriendly."

Tommy squirmed in his chair and began to protest over

36

what Frank said. Didn't Tommy know? thought Wesley; didn't he know what Frank was doing?

"Who's unfriendly?" the plump girl asked indignantly.

"You haven't even told us your names," Frank answered. He said it as though he were pouting.

The plump girl looked around as if she were afraid of the punishment that might come to her if she gave their names to these four boys from Montana.

"I'm Anna. This is Beverly."

Lester got up and angrily pushed his chair back to the table. "Enough of this shit. I'm going to see if we can't get some food out here."

"Last names," said Frank. "What are your last names?"

Anna pointed to her friend. "Tuttle." She put her hand up by her throat. "Tall Horse. Anna Tall Horse." Wesley noticed a blush rising to her cheeks when she said her name. Only when she spoke her name did her smile diminish, as if the act of naming herself required all the seriousness she could summon.

Tommy said, "Tall Horse, huh. I believe I could ride a tall horse. Get those stirrups adjusted and it don't matter how high or low the horse is." He burst into laughter. Then he lifted his boot high enough for everyone to see. "But I ain't wearing spurs. You got nothing to worry about."

"Jesus, Tommy," Wesley said.

"Jesus yourself. You ain't getting us anywhere. Why don't you go with Lester and see about getting the grub."

Wesley looked over at Beverly Tuttle. If she heard him try to intercede on behalf of her and her friend, she gave no sign.

She kept right on staring out the window, though Wesley knew there was nothing for her to see but blowing snow and a late afternoon that couldn't hold its light against all the forces that wanted to shut it down.

I'm not like them, he wanted to say. They're just after you to see what they can tear off you or stick in you. They don't even see how beautiful you are; they don't even care. But I— I'd be happy to just stare at you. I don't want to hurt you or take advantage of you. You can trust me. You can talk to me. . . . But hot on the heels of those thoughts came these: Wesley knew he wasn't going to speak to Beverly. And he knew she wouldn't see him as any different from his brother and his friends. Why should she? For although he held these noble impulses toward Beverly he also wished that she would come back to the hotel with them, that she would drink so much of their whiskey that she would let them—Wesley included—do what they wanted to her. Wesley closed his eyes and dropped his head into his hands, wishing he could squeeze from his mind all but the nobler thoughts.

When he lifted his head and opened his eyes, Tommy was putting the matter directly to Anna. "You come back to the hotel with us and we'll give you a drink of whiskey. What do you say to that?"

She was shaking her head no, but Wesley thought her smile said she was not entirely averse to the proposal.

By now Frank had slid his chair over so that he was sitting closer to the girls' table than his own. "What are you saying?" he said to Tommy. "These are Sacred Heart girls. Sacred Heart girls don't drink whiskey." He smiled wickedly at Anna. "Do they?"

"You got a moving picture here?" asked Tommy. "We could take you to the moving picture."

Anna shook her head. "There's one over in Henton."

"You been?"

She shook her head again.

"Want to go? How far's Henton? We can drive over to Henton to see a moving picture. You gals come on over to the hotel with us and we'll take you to Henton."

"Tonight?"

"Or don't Sacred Heart girls go to the moving pictures either?" asked Tommy.

"In the snow?"

"We drove in, didn't we? How far's Henton?"

"She's got a boyfriend," Anna said, nodding in Beverly's direction.

Tommy looked to the right and the left. "Where? I don't see him."

Anna lowered her voice. "They're going to get married."

"Well, they're not getting married tonight, are they?" said Frank.

"I'd think she'd want to be with a cowboy before she was married," Tommy said. "Once anyway. Find out what she was missing."

"Jesus Christ," Wesley said. "She's sitting right there."

"You better watch your mouth there, brother. These are Sacred Heart girls."

"Watch my mouth? Did you hear what he said?"

Anna wagged her finger in Tommy's direction. "If her

boyfriend heard you talk. . . ." She shook her head gravely.

"Am I supposed to be scared?" asked Tommy.

Anna's voice shifted and became like a little girl's. "He's coming to pick us up."

"In a car?" asked Frank. "Or a wagon?"

Without taking her eyes from the window, Beverly spoke up. "He's got a truck."

In a falsetto, Tommy said, "A truck. He's got a truck."

"As soon as she graduates," Anna volunteered. "That's when they're getting married."

Tommy reached into his coat pocket. "We got to do something about this boyfriend."

Frank leaned toward Beverly. "You're awful young to be an old married woman."

Tommy dropped the pistol on the tabletop and gave it a spin. The gun rumbled on the wood like far-off thunder. As it slowed, Anna and the boys watched to see where the barrel would finally point. It stopped—aimed just to the left of Tommy—and Wesley saw it clearly.

It was a .38 revolver, nickel plated, but the plating had worn off in so many places the gun was as black as it was silver. The black checkered grip was partially broken off and exposed the steel and the screw of the handle.

Wesley had seen it before. It was Tommy's pistol—he had won it in a poker game from a classmate—and a sorry one at that. The cylinder wobbled and didn't always line up the cartridge just right, and the action was so balky that the hammer might not fall with sufficient force to fire the gun. Frank had warned Tommy about the gun, telling him that it might blow up in his hand someday or send lead spraying out that loose cylinder.

All of them except Lester had handguns, and occasionally they brought them on a hunting trip so they could do a little target shooting with them or practice drawing and shooting from the hip. But they did not carry them into town, and they did not bring them into cafes.

Tommy picked up the pistol and held it loosely by his ear. "Now where's this boyfriend?"

"How long you been carrying that?" asked Frank.

"Right along."

Wesley twisted around in his chair, trying to get a better look at the gun. He wanted to see the end of the cylinder, to see if there were nothing there but black empty chambers or if there were the dark glinting nubs of bullets.

Anna said, "You better not let Mrs. Spitzer see you with that."

Tommy sighted the gun out the window. "Do I wait for him to come in or should I drop him as soon as he drives up?"

"I don't believe that will be necessary," Frank said. There was a pitch of nervousness in his brother's voice that Wesley hadn't heard before.

Wesley didn't want to look away from Tommy but he stole a glance at Beverly. She was sitting as still as ever, her hands on her lap, her eyes fixed on the street. She reminded Wesley of an old woman in Bentrock, Mrs. Gamble, who spent so many long hours in her porch swing—just sitting, not reading or sewing or shelling peas or counting rosary beads—that sitting came to seem an act of great endurance.

41

Tommy swung the pistol away from the window, and, just as he had earlier with an imaginary rifle, sighted in on the buffalo. "What do you bet I can take out one of those glass eyes?"

"You fire that thing in here," said Frank, "and we'll never get waited on."

At that moment Lester returned to the table. He had seen Tommy waving the gun about. "Yeah, shoot up the place. That'd be real fucking smart."

"Come on," said Wesley. "These girls."

Then, as though neither gun nor girls were there, as though he were simply speaking to his three hungry friends, as in fact he was, Lester said, "I ordered you all fried ham sandwiches and tomato soup. If that ain't what you want, you go tell her. She's back there making pies. The other lady didn't come in today because of the weather. That's how come she didn't take our order right away. She's doing it all herself."

Frank had slid even closer to Anna, and, hunched over in his chair, he was talking softly to her, low and steady, and while he spoke he flicked his finger up and down on the hem of her dress. The motion looked idle, playful, unconscious, but each time he moved his finger her dress rode a fraction of an inch higher on her brown leg and then fell again. "Maybe you could show us your school," he said. "Or where do you like to go? I'd like to see. Or we can go back to the hotel. . . . Keep us company. Tell us what it's like in this part of North Dakota. . . ." He nodded in Beverly's direction. "She doesn't have to come. If she's worried about her boyfriend getting jealous. I understand. I don't have a girlfriend myself right now, but I know how it is. . . ."

42

Something moved outside. Wesley turned his head and saw the truck, suddenly there in front of the Buffalo Cafe, the smoke of the exhaust whipping away in the wind. The truck's side window was frosted over, and Wesley couldn't see the driver.

Beverly saw the truck too, and she jumped from her chair with amazing speed. She grabbed her friend's arm and tried to pull her from her chair. "Let's *go!*" Beverly said.

But her friend didn't get up fast enough, and as Beverly went past, Tommy reached for her. He caught her by the coat, pulling it halfway off one arm. She tried to twist away from him, and her own grasp on her friend gave way just as Tommy released her.

Whatever the cause—her own momentum, or a wet spot on the floor where snow from someone's shoe or boot had melted into a puddle, or a kinked corner of a rug, or Tommy's foot thrust out to trip her up—Beverly fell, and fell hard. One arm had been occupied grabbing her friend and the other tangled in her coat, so she didn't have time to get her hands under her to break her fall. She landed headfirst. The thud was as loud as a chair toppling over, and Wesley felt the floorboards vibrate.

Anna bent to help her friend, but before she could touch her Beverly was on her feet again and running toward the door, towing Anna behind her.

With both Frank and Tommy shouting after them, the girls ran from the cafe, slamming the door behind them. The glass rattled in the door, and the bell continued to ring nervously long after they went out.

Wesley watched them run to the truck. Anna stumbled in the street and almost slipped under the front of the truck, but Beverly jerked her upright and both of them scrambled into the cab of the truck. Their door wasn't even shut before the truck began to move off.

They were out of sight before Wesley felt the chill that had entered the cafe when the door opened.

"Lookit!" said Lester. "Look what you did waving your goddamn gun around." He pointed over by the door. One of Anna's oversized galoshes stood there, right where the girl must have stepped out of it in her haste to get out of the cafe.

"You scared her right out of her fucking boots," Lester said and laughed.

Then it was Frank's turn to point. His finger was aimed at the floor where Beverly had fallen. A six-inch smear of blood glistened against the wood.

Wesley stood. He had no idea where he was going or what he was going to do; he just knew he needed to move.

"She might as well be gone then," Tommy said. "We got no use for her if she's on the rag." He couldn't hold his straight face any longer, and he broke up with laughter.

Frank looked up at his brother. "Where you going this time?"

"I don't know. . . ."

"Sit down then. I told you before. We're not in the jurisdiction."

Lester had gotten up too. He went over to the blood spot, bent over, and stared closely at it. "Do you think that's what it is?"

44

"Where the hell's the food?" asked Tommy. He picked up the salt shaker, sprinkled salt over his gun, and pretended to take a bite from the barrel. He chewed for a while then slipped the pistol back into his coat pocket.

"You can still fuck 'em when they're on the rag," Frank said.

"Kind of messy," Tommy said as if he were wise in these matters.

"Hey, I'm having the tomato soup," protested Lester.

"My dad arrested a man for murder a few years back," Frank said. "Or manslaughter or something. Fellow busted in on this woman, an old girlfriend or maybe she used to be his wife. He was planning on screwing her but then he found out she had her period. He flipped her over and did her up the ass. Then someone found her dead. Big mystery. Dad figured it out. When this fellow had her pinned down he pushed her face into the pillow. Smothered her. Maybe they got him for rape *and* murder. Some such."

"Was this an Indian gal?" asked Tommy.

"I don't believe so. They sent him up for life in Deer Lodge."

Lester couldn't stop shaking his head. "Who was the fellow?"

"Some Frenchy. Down from Canada, I believe. Wasn't from Montana."

Tommy moved his coat to shift the weight of the gun in his pocket. "That's probably how them Canucks like it."

"Dad told you that story?" Wesley asked his brother.

"Yep."

45

"When?"

"I don't know. A year or two ago. We were going some-where in the car. I don't remember."

"He never told me."

"So? I just did."

Wesley couldn't be sure what shocked him more, the story with its mingling of sex and murder, overlaid with sodomy, an act whose existence was known to him and his friends but rarely spoken of, even in their willingness, their eagerness, to discuss almost all matters sexual, or the fact that the story came from his father.

Julian Hayden was a man who swore freely and made no attempt to rein in his tongue in the presence of his sons, but his talk—overrun as it was with profanity—was free of sexual references. As Frank himself once said, their father's speech was shit-covered but fuck-free.

Now this story. Wesley felt he had to readjust not only his view of his father and his work, but also of his father's attitude toward him. Why could his father tell this story to Frank but not to his younger son?

The gray-haired woman came out from the kitchen carry-ing a platter of food. "I wasn't sure," she said as she approached their table, "if you boys got so tired of waiting you up and left. Or if maybe you just dried up from hunger."

Wesley looked again at the blood on the floor. Would she see it?

She put the soup bowls down first, then the small crockery plates holding the sandwiches of fried ham between slices of diagonally sliced white bread. Finally she put down spoons.

"I'll get you some milk," she said but made no move to walk away. "As soon as the pies are done I'll bring you each a piece. Free, for making you wait so long."

They began to eat while she stood there, watching them intently as though her pleasure depended upon seeing others consume her fare.

She crossed her arms. "Them girls' ride come?" Without waiting for an answer, she nodded. "I just don't like for them to use my phone like that."

They sat quietly on the floor of their hotel, smoking cigars and sipping whiskey. They were pleased with their behavior, and often in the last two hours, ever since they arrived back in the room, one of them had commented on their maturity, on how they were able to enjoy a glass of whiskey for its taste rather than simply drinking to get drunk as many of their peers would do. Wesley, however, had begun to feel shivery and unsteady from the drink. He knew if he closed his eyes he might topple over into sleep.

They had long since stopped discussing the Indian girls. The argument finally ended when Frank, conceded as the authority on such matters, announced that it was not Tommy bringing out the gun that ruined their chances with the girls but the fact of Beverly's boyfriend. As long as she insisted on remaining loyal to him, she could not be persuaded to come with them. And Anna would not come without her friend. "Sacred Heart didn't help either," Wesley added.

"No, it sure didn't," agreed his brother.

When the knock came, it was so soft—three taps almost like brush strokes—Wesley thought, and he was sure the others did too, that they had been wrong. The girls had decided to come after all! Tommy jumped to his feet to answer the door, while Lester had the presence of mind to cork the whiskey and roll it under the bed and to throw his coat over their glasses.

Standing in the doorway was a portly man of average height wearing a wool overcoat with a black mouton collar. Visible beneath his open coat was a three-piece suit of heavy salt-and-pepper tweed, white shirt, and tie. He wore a fedora tilted back. His large moon face was split by a wide smile.

As soon as the door opened, the man lifted his hand in a casual salute. "Howdy, boys." His voice was as high pitched and soft as a woman's.

Wesley could see why the knock on the door was so faint. The man wore bright yellow buckskin mittens with fur-lined cuffs that came halfway up his forearms. Wesley had seen similar mittens, designed especially for hunters, but the ones he had seen had the trigger finger cut free. The man's rimless spectacles were well down his nose; no doubt he had tilted them down when he came in out of the cold and they steamed up in the sudden warmth of the hotel. "I'm Sheriff Cooke," he said. "And might you be the boys from Montana?"

In the silence that followed only Wesley was able to find his tongue. "That's us," he said. As soon as he spoke he felt as though he had already admitted to some guilt.

Sheriff Cooke stepped into the room alone, but Wesley

felt as though others were with him. Once Wesley got to his feet and looked into the hall he saw his intuition was right.

Two men in wool caps waited a few yards down the hall. They faced the open door and stood with their legs spread wide as if they were prepared to block the way. One of the men wore a long belted overcoat that looked as though it might at one time have been military issue. The other man wore a short wool jacket, and he was carrying a rifle or shotgun. Wesley didn't know for certain because the gun was in a cloth scabbard. He cradled the gun loosely in his arms.

Sheriff Cooke waved his hand in front of him as if to clear the air. "Better pull on your boots, boys. I'm going to have you come with me."

"What's the trouble, sir?" Frank asked.

The sheriff kept waving his hand, and now he began to sniff the air as well. "You suppose you could spare one of those cigars?"

Wesley wondered if this might be a trick of some kind—first they would admit to smoking cigars and next he would inquire about the whiskey.

Tommy, however, had already reached into the box and was handing a cigar to the sheriff.

Sheriff Cooke held the cigar to his nose and inhaled deeply. "You won't need your coats. We don't have that far to walk." He put the cigar in his coat pocket and led the way out of the hotel room.

Wesley had a momentary impulse to hang back and then slam and lock the door behind the sheriff's back. Then—then what? Leap from the window? Wait for the sheriff and his

49

deputies to crash through the door and drag him out? Frank followed the sheriff, and Wesley fell in behind his brother.

The sheriff's office was not at all what Wesley expected. Their own father's office was in the basement of Mercer County courthouse, a large stone building fronted by a long flight of steps leading to heavy glass doors between massive fluted columns. The Great Northern depot was the only public building in Bentrock older than the courthouse.

McCoy, North Dakota, had its sheriff's office and county jail in a small, simple one-story building made of the same orange brick as the hotel.

The boys had walked coatless the length of McCoy's main street, and though the snow had stopped and the wind died down, the temperature had continued to drop. The wind-packed snow crunched underfoot, and their breath formed great clouds of steam. They thrust their hands deep into their pockets or wrapped their arms around themselves trying to make smaller targets for the cold. Once inside the jail they relaxed their shoulders and raised their eyes to examine their surroundings.

The jail's interior was as plain as the exterior. There was a desk and swivel chair, a long bench that could at one time have been a church pew, and a coal stove with its pipe extending sideways through the wall. An empty electric light socket hung from the ceiling, and the room's only light came from two kerosene lamps with soot-blackened chimneys. A telephone and a gun rack hung on the wall by the door. As Sheriff Cooke led them into his office he asked cheerfully, "What do you think, boys—down below zero yet?"

"Ten below, I bet," Tommy said.

"Wouldn't doubt it. Wouldn't doubt it one bit."

The two men from the hotel had filed into the jail behind the boys. The one in the jacket leaned his gun against the wall by the door. Wesley hadn't heard either man speak, and now they stood by the door as if awaiting orders.

Sheriff Cooke pointed to the bench across from his desk. "Why don't you boys sit yourselves down right over there." He dropped his weight into the swivel chair, which gave out a rusty whine.

Sheriff Cooke nodded to the men by the door. "You can go take care of matters back there." They left the jail immediately, and the shorter man left his gun behind.

Wesley could see inside a back room the bars of jail cells.

"They're not both deputies," Sheriff Cooke explained. "Just Mr. Rawlins in the overcoat. Mr. Rozinski lends us a hand now and then." He chuckled in a way that caused the loose flesh of his jowls to vibrate. "When we've got more outlaws on our hands than we can handle."

"Maybe you could tell us what you think we did," said Tommy.

The sheriff didn't answer for a long time. He reached into his desk drawer and took out a tin of Velvet tobacco and a packet of rolling papers. He took his time rolling his cigarette, as if he were a man who did not smoke often and so wanted each cigarette to be as well made as possible. He moistened the paper not by drawing it the length of his tongue but by flicking out his tongue in tiny licks.

When the wooden match flared, Wesley jumped. He knew then that he was not simply frightened but still a little drunk.

"You have pie over at the cafe?" Sheriff Cooke asked them.

"Yes," answered Frank.

"What's she serving today?"

"We had apple."

Sheriff Cooke nodded as though Frank was merely verifying something the sheriff already knew. "If there's someone on the face of this earth who bakes a better pie than Florence Spitzer, I'd like to know who. You did right having pie at the Buffalo Cafe. . . ."

Wesley thought the sheriff was going to go on and say, "But you did wrong when you——" but his soft high voice just faded away and he fell silent, rocking in his squeaking chair, smoking, and eyeing the boys seated on the bench in front of him.

Tommy broke the silence. "How long do we have to stay here?" His question was straightforward, without any note of pleading or whining that Wesley could detect.

Sheriff Cooke answered with a gesture. He swiveled around in his chair and motioned for them to come near. "I want to show you something."

They stepped over to the wall Sheriff Cooke was facing. There, along with a Soo Line calendar and some Wanted circulars, were photographs and clippings from newspapers. The sheriff tapped one of the pictures. "Look right here at this one."

In the yellow newspaper photograph a group of fifteen or twenty people, mostly men in suits and ties, stood or sat around a table set up outdoors for a ceremony of some sort. In the center of the group was a broad-shouldered, dark-skinned, bareheaded Indian in deerskin leggings and a beaded shirt. The Indian had a bow pulled back to full draw and his nocked arrow was aimed at the sky. A few of the people in the photograph looked at the Indian but most stared at the camera.

Sheriff Cooke stood behind the boys so they could get a better look at the clipping.

The caption under the photograph read, "Sioux warrior Iron Hail became an American citizen at Fort Duncan, North Dakota. As part of the ceremony, Iron Hail released an arrow into the air and said, 'I shoot my last arrow.'"

The sheriff tapped the photograph in the vicinity of the table. "Yours truly." He straightened up and Wesley felt the sheriff's hand rest on his shoulder. "And do you recognize that old warrior?"

Wesley and his friends leaned in, as though any face there could be known to them if they only stared hard enough. Every man and woman in the photograph stared impassively at the camera, their eyes as blank and dark as stones. Only because he had been told that Sheriff Cooke was in the picture could Wesley see any resemblance between the full-moon face in the picture and the man behind him.

Frank was the first to turn away from the wall. "I don't know anybody there."

The sheriff chuckled softly, a sound a little like footsteps

53

creaking on snow. "Well, you might say you do. Yessir. You do."

He tapped the photograph again. "Iron Hail is now George Tuttle. Took an American name when he became a citizen. Or they gave it to him. Whichever. Is there a date on there? This was in the *Bismarck Tribune*. Back in 1917. Of course they're all citizens now, whether they want to be or not. You boys can go sit back down."

The sheriff returned to his chair and fell into another long pause. Wesley was most uneasy during these silences. He was afraid one of them would blurt out a confession. His father had often told them how, when some people were arrested, they would simply begin talking, even admitting to crimes with which they were not going to be charged. "They can't carry all that guilt," his father would say, "and first chance they get they dump the whole load."

Wesley understood. He felt that ache for release, and he had to clamp his jaw down hard. Talking was all he could do in this situation, and that was something he felt he could do tolerably well. Hadn't he been told for years, by his mother, his teachers, his grandmother, that he was a good boy, bright, polite, and well spoken? If he simply started talking he could explain everything—with a half-truth, half-lie concoction the sheriff would surely swallow—how they had the whiskey, where they got the cigars, why Tommy had a pistol in the Buffalo Cafe, what they wanted with those girls. But his father's words kept coming back. "If they'd keep their goddamn mouths shut, half these people would get off scot-free."

Those *girls!* Oh Jesus! Beverly Tuttle. George Tuttle.

As if he were reading Wesley's thoughts, Sheriff Cooke said, "Yessir. Mr. Tuttle. That's the papa of the girl you knocked down over at the cafe."

Tommy was quick to defend himself. "She *fell!*"

"Bloodied her up pretty good. Chipped a tooth. Cut her lip bad. Almost bit right through it." Sheriff Cooke shuddered a little as though the thought of Beverly Tuttle's injury chilled him.

"How'd she get the scar?" The question sprang out of Wesley before he even knew it was near his tongue.

"She didn't need any more problems in that area, did she?" said the sheriff. "Poor gal. As I recall, she got that in a sledding accident. Went flying down a hill headed right toward a barbed wire fence. Tried laying back so she could squeak under it and a strand caught her by the lip." He shuddered again. "Such a pretty gal."

Frank added quickly, as though, the door finally open, everyone could contribute an explanation or excuse. "We didn't mean for her to get hurt."

"She slipped," Tommy repeated.

Sheriff Cooke leaned forward and twined his fingers as if he were going to pray. "Course you didn't mean for her to get hurt. Pretty gal like that. I'm sure you had other ideas."

Frank interrupted him. "We didn't want that—"

"—and I believe you. I know where you're from. Montana's full of good people. But here you are now. In my jurisdiction. Waving guns around. Drinking whiskey. Bothering the gals here in town. Indian or not. What do you suppose the boys here think about you coming around after their gals?

55

They'd like to chase you down, I bet. You're lucky I got you here where they can't get to you."

Lester spoke for the first time since they had entered the jail, and his voice had a pace and sonority that Wesley hadn't heard before. "We ain't scared."

"Course you're not. No. You wouldn't be here if you were. But I'm thinking about another matter right now. Trying to figure out what I'm going to do."

"You could just let us go," suggested Tommy.

Wesley stared at the floor. He wished Tommy would keep quiet.

"Could. I could." He leaned back in his chair and stared at the ceiling as if he were deep in thought.

Frank was staring at Wesley, and Wesley raised his eyebrows to question what his brother wanted. Frank did not move, speak, or change his grave expression. Wesley mouthed the word, "What?" Frank looked away.

Sheriff Cooke carefully placed his palms on his desk and pushed himself up. "Tell you what. You boys go back there." He pointed toward the jail area. "Wait on me back there. Just shut the door behind you. That's right. Right through there."

The door they closed behind them was thick wood, so dark it looked fire blackened, and its heavy brass latch clicked shut like the lock on a gate. Each of the three open cells had an iron bunk and an overhead light socket in a wire cage, but there were no bulbs in any of the fixtures. The only light came from a corner in the back where a floor lamp stood. With its crenellated pedestal and opaque glass shade it looked like something that belonged in a parlor.

"Shit," Lester said. "Now what?"

Wesley's father's jail usually smelled of disinfectant, but this area stank of urine and mold. The cement walls had large dark spots, permanent sweat stains from seeping moisture. "Feels like we're underground," said Wesley.

"Why didn't you tell him who your old man is?" Tommy asked.

"What for?" Frank replied.

"Jesus. Maybe Sheriff Cooke might let us go, that's what for."

"I don't think that would cut it with Mr. Cooke."

"You don't think. You could tell him and see what happens."

Lester wandered into one of the cells. "Fucking Indian bitches. What do you suppose they did? Hightail it over here first thing?"

"What would your old man do to us?" Tommy asked Wesley and Frank. "If we was in his county."

Frank turned to his brother. "What do you think? Just shoot us and bury us, don't you reckon?"

"Probably wouldn't even bother with the burying."

"I bet it was the boyfriend," said Lester from the cell. "Couldn't fight his own battles so he runs to the sheriff."

"Can you imagine," Tommy said, "what your dad would do if we came to him to take care of our problems?"

Lester found a slop bucket, an enameled pot that he dragged out into the middle of the cell. He lifted the lid, spread his legs and urinated, the stream hissing and ringing off the metal. "But if he heard someone was waving a gun around in Roller's Cafe he'd sure as hell come running."

"That he would," agreed Frank.

Lester covered the pot and slid it back under the bunk. He kept staring down at his fly, as if he weren't quite convinced he had buttoned it correctly. "Maybe you should've told him who your pa is though."

Frank nodded at Tommy. "Maybe *he* should've kept that gun in his goddamn pocket."

Wesley weighed in on his brother's side. "Maybe he should've left it in the goddamn room."

Tommy aimed a listless kick in Wesley's direction, and as he did, Frank shoved him, sending Tommy stumbling into the wall. Tommy let himself be carried further than the push's actual force warranted. "Fine," said Tommy. "I don't give a good goddamn. Go ahead and put this on me."

"Nobody's putting it all on you," Frank said. "We're just saying, you're the one had the gun."

"Well, the sheriff didn't say too much about a gun."

"Figures though, don't it," added Lester.

Tommy rubbed the floor with the toe of his boot and then spit toward that spot. "Shit ass."

Frank squatted against the wall, leaning his head back and trying to make himself as comfortable as he could. "And you can leave off that business, telling him who our dad is. We're not going to do it."

Wesley sat next to his brother and looked at his companions.

Each stared at a far wall or into a dark corner as though he was waiting for something in the room's shadows to take shape and lead them out of their predicament.

On the floor in front of Wesley was a small dark stain. He wondered if blood could have made that mark, and then he tried to push that thought away by concentrating on the stain's shape. Iowa? Was that its shape? Like the state of Iowa on a map of the United States? Their father originally came from Iowa, and whenever he looked at a map Wesley liked to estimate the distance between Iowa and Montana. Or maybe rust made that stain.

Wesley held his head very still, trying to determine if he was still feeling the whiskey. The stain didn't move, and neither did his head, even when a drop of icy nervous sweat fell from his armpit to his ribs. He was sober, for all the good it did him.

His shoulder still held the memory of Sheriff Cooke's hand resting there. His hand had felt warm, tender, and for the few seconds it rested on his shoulder Wesley could allow himself to believe that the sheriff meant them no harm.

None of the cells had windows, but there was a small high window at the other end of the jail. Wesley considered going down there, hoisting himself up, and looking out. What would he see? Another wall? Snow, certainly. Snow, snow, and more snow.

Three years ago in late December, right before Christmas, warm chinook winds rolled down the Rockies' eastern slopes, pushing temperatures into the forties and fifties. For five days the western winds blew, and when they stopped there wasn't a patch of snow left in northeast Montana. Women went coatless, men gathered in the streets in their shirtsleeves, and the town skating rink turned into a pond of slush. Boys threw baseballs in the streets and their fathers went out to the golf course.

That Christmas Wesley was in love with Martha Woods, a girl in the class ahead of him at school. Martha didn't know of Wesley's feelings for her; in fact, they had no relationship at all beyond saying hello on the streets or in the halls of their school. Nevertheless, as that warm, gusty, snowless Christmas approached, Wesley felt he had to do something to declare his feelings for Martha. At Douglas's Rexall he bought her a gift, a perfumed powder puff and mirror set, and he took it to her house on the afternoon of Christmas Eve.

As Wesley stood on the porch of the Woods home and waited for Martha to appear, he could hear the warm wind rattling the house's rain gutters and humming through the window casements. Snowmelt ran through the streets like bright new rivers.

At last Martha appeared, but she was with a friend, and the small speech Wesley had prepared could not be delivered in front of another listener. He thrust the package out to Martha, and he saw now how sloppily he had wrapped it—the uneven ends, the crumpled and creased paper, the drooping ribbon. He said, "For you, a Christmas gift"—a phrase that sounded ridiculously formal. No one talked that way! At least no one in Bentrock, Montana.

Martha took the package and she smiled at Wesley, a smile that told him in an instant exactly how she felt about him. She thought he was a foolish boy, and though she thanked him extravagantly, it was plain she received this offering the way a mother or older sister would accept a gift from a five-year-old son or brother.

As soon as the package was out of his hands Wesley backed away, and he got off the porch quickly so he would not have to hear the laughter of Martha and her friend.

He trudged home, soaking his boots in the water and slush that filled the gutters and streets of Bentrock on Christmas of 1921.

He thought that day that he would never again experience a Christmas like those of his childhood—stealing his mother's cookies, opening the expensive gifts from his father, pushing through the crowd of friends and neighbors who often filled the house, listening to his mother play the piano and sing carols, sledding and skating with his brother—all that innocence and joy seemed to vanish with the melting snow.

But maybe those Christmases could come back if only the snow would return. . . . Since that day, snow never fell without Wesley thinking, at least for a moment, that it was a fulfillment of his wish.

Yet tonight Wesley and his brother and their friends sat in the McCoy jail because snow filled up the fields and sloughs, the hills and ravines, the highways and trails of Montana and North Dakota.

The jail's floor was not much warmer than the frozen ground the building sat upon, and the cold worked its way up Wesley's spine until his entire body was wired tight. Nevertheless, he stayed where he was; he was too tired to stand up and move around, and he'd be damned if he'd go into one of the cells, even if it did have a bunk to sit on.

"Anybody got a watch?" asked Lester. "How long we been in here?"

Wesley reached for the pocket where he usually kept his watch. Then he remembered Frank's instruction: on a hunting trip you leave your watch at home.

"I don't know. A couple hours," Frank said.

"Maybe this is it," suggested Tommy. "Maybe he's going to keep us here a while then let us go."

"Maybe," Frank replied.

"But you don't think so."

"I didn't say that."

"But do you," Tommy pressed, "do you think he'll just let us go? I mean, we been here a while."

"I don't have an opinion," answered Frank. "Why the hell you keep asking me?"

"Because your old man's a sheriff!"

"Not here he ain't." Frank's face was flushed with anger, and Tommy let the subject drop. Instead, he raised a new issue.

"I don't get it," Tommy said. "So she's the daughter of this old Sioux warrior. What the hell does that mean? This sheriff has to protect her or something? I never heard of such."

"Wonder who her boyfriend is," Lester mused.

"White, do you think?" Tommy asked.

Frank was bent over, studying the door latch. "I wouldn't be surprised."

"It ain't even got a lock," Wesley told his brother.

"I can see that."

"'I shoot my last arrow,'" said Tommy. "What kind of bullshit is that?"

Frank and Lester both laughed. "Indian bullshit," Frank said.

"He didn't say he shot his last bullet," added Lester. "Or stoled his last horse. Or rustled his last cow. Or took his last scalp. Or slit his last throat."

"Or drank his last whiskey," Tommy said.

Wesley couldn't join in. Iron Hail's words were still running around his mind, and Wesley found them thrillingly poetic. He knew he would remember them to the end of his days. He wished the day would come when he could repeat it himself. Perhaps he'd be a soldier someday and perform an act of heroism. Lying gravely wounded on the battlefield, Wesley would look up at the comrades whom he'd just rescued and say, "Friends, like old Iron Hail once said, 'I've shot my last arrow.'" If he could have walked Beverly Tuttle home through the snow, he would have shaken her father's hand and said, "Sir, I'm proud to know you." Then Wesley's thoughts cleared: If he would have walked Beverly home, he never would have landed in jail. And he wouldn't know of the ceremony honoring Iron Hail.

"Well, I guess the old Indian's somebody around these parts," Wesley said to his friends.

"Oh hell yes," said Lester. "He's a citizen."

"You never know," Frank said. "Maybe they got a shortage of citizens."

Sheriff Cooke swung open the door with such force that the heavy door banged against the wall and woke Lester, who had fallen asleep sitting on the floor. "Up and at 'em, boys," the sheriff said. "Rise and shine."

Sheriff Cooke had his gloves and overcoat back on, buttoned to the throat. Behind him in the office was Deputy Rawlins, his gun once again cradled in his arms. Now, however, it was out of its scabbard, and Wesley and the others could see what kind of a weapon it was. Winchester .30-.30, lever action Model 94, just like the rifle Frank had brought on this hunting trip. Wesley couldn't be sure—was his heart beating faster from jumping to his feet after Sheriff Cooke threw open the door or from the sight of the gun unsheathed?

"Follow me, boys," Sheriff Cooke said and led them from the cell area, through the office, and toward the jail's front door. Just as he had done when they left the hotel, the deputy fell in behind the four boys.

They walked past the bench where they had sat earlier, and Wesley saw something that frightened him more than the deputy's rifle. There, lined up on the bench, was all their gear from the hotel—their hats and coats, their duffels and packs, sleeping bags, rifles, shotguns, and ammunition, everything they had brought in from the car. On top of the pile was the bright red and green box of La Playa cigars with the picture of the beautiful senorita smiling out from under her mantilla. Wesley guessed their whiskey was sitting in a drawer of Sheriff Cooke's desk. Wesley was the last in line, and his brother was right in front of him. As they filed past their belongings, Frank turned around to

Wesley and said, "You stay close."

Outside the wind had died and now the night was so still you could hear a dog barking far off—asking, no doubt, to be let in. Much closer was the rhythmic scrape of someone shoveling snow.

Wesley knew why none of them asked where they were going. Because as long as they didn't know, they could pretend that everything would be all right once they arrived.

The little troupe turned into a narrow alley between the jail and a brick building next door. As they entered the alley Wesley could see the sign painted on the side of the building, its black letters stenciled on a white background and lit by a single light hanging over the sign. "CHOICE LIQUORS. Beeler's Liquor Store. Pool Hall in Connection. McCoy, No. Dak." Wesley wondered how thickly the snow would have to fall, how hard the wind blow, before those words would be obscured. Could a blizzard be so strong that you could stand in this alley and be unable to read that sign?

The shoveling came from halfway down the alley, where Cooke's other deputy was clearing the snow from an area the size of a small room. As he shoveled, he stacked the snow into a large bank against the wall of the liquor store. A lantern sat on the ground nearby, and the light coming from below made it look as though the shoveler had uncovered something, under the first layers of snow, that gave off a strange glow.

Sheriff Cooke called out, "That's sufficient, Clarence."

The sheriff marched the boys down the alley until they came to the cleared area. "Right here," he said, indicating that they should line up facing the snowbank. "This'll do fine."

Wesley peered down to the other end of the alley. It looked like a car was parked there, blocking the space between the buildings. Was that their car? He glanced back in the direction from which they had just come, to the opening in the alley. Now that too seemed further away. Sometimes snow could trick you about distances. Blowing, it could make even close objects look far away. Stacked up deep, snow could make walking even a hundred yards seem as tiring as a mile.

If he ran—no, no, when he ran—Wesley wondered which way he would go: toward the light or toward the car.

"Who's going first here?" Sheriff Cooke asked as cheerfully as a schoolteacher searching for volunteers in the classroom.

The man who followed them out of the jail now faced them, a man with a gun and a man with a shovel each standing to one side of the snowbank.

A firing squad, Wesley thought. That's what this is. They're going to line us up and shoot us one by one and let our bodies fall back onto the snow. And with that thought a strange calm came over him. He hadn't done anything to deserve being shot. None of them had. Not today in McCoy. Not ever. That didn't lessen his conviction that they were going to be shot, but it made it easier to bear. Sheriff Cooke was going to have them executed, and he was wrong for doing it. They weren't wholly innocent, but in death they would be redeemed, victims of this great injustice.

"Looks like you're the one," Sheriff Cooke said, pointing to Tommy for no other reason than that he was at the end of the line and closest to the sheriff. Tommy, Lester, Frank, Wesley. . . . Wesley counted off as if he were in Sunday

School trying to determine how many others would have to recite the Bible verse before Mrs. McDougall called on him.

"What for?" asked Tommy.

"What for? That's the wrong question, young man. We're out here now, and we're going to proceed. You can get us started here by pulling down your pants. Both your trousers and your drawers."

Whether from cold or fear or both, Wesley began to shiver. Once the shaking began it would soon take him over completely, and Wesley was afraid he would have no control over any part of his being—not his voice, his breath, his bowels. He tried something else. He relaxed his jaw and set his teeth chattering as fast as they would go. If his body wanted to tremble, he would allow it this much. And as long as his teeth kept up this machine-gun clatter echoing inside his skull, he still had some control.

"I ain't dropping my drawers out here," Tommy said. "Not in this cold."

"That's exactly what you're going to do. And then we'll proceed from there."

"No sir."

"Or we can cut them off you. And I can't promise you we can see any too well where the knife's going in out here in the dark."

"What're you going to do?" Tommy asked as he reached for his belt.

Wesley heard the clink of Tommy's heavy metal belt buckle. Wesley didn't have any idea what Sheriff Cooke had in mind either, but he knew he'd rather be shot than have something done to him with his pants down.

"I told you," the sheriff said. "Drawers too."

"Jesus," Tommy said, and now his voice was trembling.

"All right," the sheriff said, as if someone had finally come up with the right answer. "You came to town looking to stick your pecker somewhere, you can stick it in that snowbank."

"The *hell*."

"Go on. Jump in there. There's no getting away from this. You don't jump in there yourself Mr. Rawlins and Mr. Rozinski are going to push you down, and you might not like the way they do it."

Out of the corner of his eye Wesley saw Tommy hobble, his pants around his knees, right up to the pile of snow.

"Let's go," Sheriff Cooke said. "Your friends are getting cold out here."

"Shit!" Tommy said, and more than leap toward the snow, he simply let himself lean and fall forward into it. He kept his arms folded in front of him; the instant his body hit he let out a shout that was half-laugh, half-cry.

Sheriff Cooke commanded, "You get up when I tell you," and at the same time the deputy with the rifle moved over and pinned Tommy down by putting his foot on his back.

"All right, Clarence," the sheriff said.

The man with the shovel braced his feet, brought his shovel back like a baseball bat, and swung. The flat back of the shovel's blade hit Tommy square on the ass, and in the cold air the metal rang like a bell, as if the shovel had met not flesh but iron. Tommy yelped like a dog, as much in surprise as in pain.

Clarence delivered four more blows, and with each one

Wesley could see Tommy's body arch and spasm with the indecision of whether to press further into the snow or to rise up and meet the shovel.

"Let him up," the sheriff said.

Tommy crawled backward out of the snowbank before getting to his feet. As soon as he stood he began frantically brushing snow from his bare skin, concentrating first on the clumps stuck in his pubic hair. He sniffled a bit, but Wesley couldn't be sure if Tommy was crying or if his nose was running from being facedown in the snow. I won't cry, Wesley resolved. They can split me open with that shovel but I won't cry.

Tommy clumsily pulled up his trousers, but his hands and fingers had too little feeling to enable him to work the belt and buckle.

Sheriff Cooke nodded at Lester. "Next."

Staring straight ahead, Lester took a long stride forward.

"I believe you know how this is proceeding. You can keep things moving by getting those trousers down right quick."

Lester's heavy wool hunting trousers were held up by suspenders and he shrugged them off his shoulders with a deft flip of his thumbs. Without looking down he began to unbutton his fly.

Lester muttered, "A spanking. A goddamn spanking. I ain't been spanked since I was six years old."

Under the snow in the alley was dirt—Wesley could see black patches of it showing through in places where the deputy had shoveled or where the wind had swept the ground clear. Nevertheless, the footing where they stood was poor—either packed snow or frozen, rutted ground—so when Lester decided to run there was a moment when his boots could find no purchase, and that slowed his sliding, skidding first step just long enough for the deputy to get his shovel up and into Lester's face.

The deputy had swung his shovel—of course he had—yet it seemed to Wesley as though all the deputy did was place the shovel in the air and Lester ran right into that square of steel.

Lester stumbled backward, his hands to his face, and then he fell, one leg bent awkwardly under him.

"God*damn* it," cursed Sheriff Cooke. Then to Rawlins and Rozinski: "Go ahead. Finish it for him."

Rawlins, with his rifle in one hand, grabbed Lester by the back of the shirt and pulled him partially to his feet. Lester's boots were moving under him but to no effect, just kicking and scrabbling uselessly on the snow. Clarence Rozinski put his shovel aside so he could work on pulling Lester's pants down.

Once his trousers were bunched around his knees, they could all see: Lester was wearing his union suit, buttoned tight throat to crotch.

"Reach in there," the sheriff said to his deputy, "and pull his pecker out for him."

"I ain't putting my hand in his drawers. No sir," Rozinski said.

Sheriff Cooke didn't ask Rawlins. He said, "Just get his face in there then. Get him cold first."

Rozinski picked up his shovel again. As if he were working

a lever, Rawlins pitched Lester face forward into the snow-bank. As soon as Lester's body hit, Rozinski had his shovel drawn back and began to administer the ringing blows, these harder, faster, and more numerous than Tommy received, perhaps to make up for the layer of cloth covering Lester's backside.

Lester lay perfectly still under the beating. Wesley wondered if he was unconscious, if something in his head had been knocked loose when he collided face first with the shovel.

Rozinski swung even harder, and Wesley hoped the deputy could keep control of his shovel. If the blade angled at all and an edge came down onto Lester it could cut into his flesh like an axe.

"That'll do," the sheriff said.

As Tommy had done, Lester crawled backwards off the snow pile, but he just kept crawling backward until he came to his place among his friends.

With Lester this close, Wesley could see the black drops in the snow from Lester's bleeding nose. Wesley traced Lester's path back to the snowdrift; yes, a trail of blood marked Lester's progress. Wesley remembered the look of Beverly Tuttle's blood staining the floor of the Buffalo Cafe. Blood for blood, Wesley thought. Was that in the Bible? No, there it was an eye for an eye. . . . Blood for blood. Where had he heard that before? He couldn't place it, yet it seemed as though he had been hearing it all his life, a saying as old as any Bible verse. Or perhaps it was not a phrase that had ever fallen on his ears. Perhaps he simply breathed it in, an attitude that was as much a part of the Montana air as the smell of sage, the feel of wind.

Lester was still on his hands and knees when he coughed twice, then vomited. He bucked hard with the force of his retching.

Wesley turned away until he could be sure Lester was finished. When he looked down he saw steam rising from the fetid pool, like a campfire just extinguished.

Sheriff Cooke put his mitten to his nose. "Whew! Throw a little snow on that, Clarence."

Clarence scooped two shovelsful of snow on top of Lester's vomit. He packed the snow down with the back of the shovel.

As he stood up, Lester staggered backward, reeling with the effort of getting his weakened body upright and his suspenders looped back over his shoulders. He kept his head tilted back to try to stanch the blood flowing from his nose.

Wesley felt something brush the front of his leg, but before he could look down to see what it was, he knew: Frank had stepped in front of him, putting his body between Sheriff Cooke and his younger brother.

The sheriff clapped his mittened hands together and let out a long cloudy breath, as if he were exhaling smoke from a cigar. "When you boys tell your daddy what went on here in McCoy, make sure you tell it right. And tell it all. He's already heard me tell the story, so you want to be damn sure your version matches up with mine. You don't want to add lying to your troubles."

Wesley realized he had been drawing such shallow breaths

that he was winded from simply standing in place. Nothing was going to happen to them. Somehow Sheriff Cooke knew—or had found out—that their father was a sheriff, another peace officer, and Cooke was letting them go. Wesley inhaled deeply, filling his lungs with air so cold it felt as though something inside him would crack.

"If you were my sons," Sheriff Cooke said to them, "I'd sit you down and give you some advice about choosing friends. Look at the trouble these two galoots got you into."

They began walking out of the alley in single file again. Lester still had his head back and his hands cupped to his nose, but Tommy had turned to face Frank and Wesley. Tommy was rubbing his arms up and down, shivering, and his face, pale with cold and anger and shame, glowed in the dark. Through his chattering teeth he said to the brothers, "You lucky fuckers."

They crested the last of a series of hills leading to Bentrock, still a good five miles from town but close enough to see the tiny scattering of lights in the valley that meant they were almost home. But this early morning, in the predawn dark, it was not the lights of town that caught their attention but the glow of a fire burning brightly just this side of the Knife River bridge, the last border separating Bentrock from all the wild country hemming in their town on every side.

"What the hell is that?" Wesley asked from the front seat.

Tommy leaned forward from the back. "What's what?"

Wesley pointed. "Out there."

"A fire?" Tommy asked. "Is that a fire?"

Lester had not spoken since they left McCoy, and in fact had slept for most of the trip, but he roused at this announcement. "What's on fire?" His voice was thick and nasal because his nostrils were packed with gauze, medical treatment that Deputy Rawlins administered back in Sheriff Cooke's office.

"Jesus," Wesley said. "What's burning?"

"Never mind," Frank answered. "I know."

"What? Can you see?" asked Tommy.

"It's Dad."

They waited then, keeping their eyes on the fire, letting its enlarging flames and brightening glow signal their progress through the night.

When they were close enough they could see, exactly as Frank had predicted, Sheriff Hayden and his deputy Len McAuley. They were parked by the bridge, their cars still partially on the road to avoid getting stuck in the deep snow drifted in the ditch. And they had built a fire, a blaze of brush and scrub wood.

Frank pulled in behind his father's car as if there was nothing unusual about parking on this empty snow-packed stretch of highway where no car had passed for hours.

Before Frank turned off the motor, Wesley saw in the glare of their headlights the silver flask his father passed back to Len McAuley. Len dropped the flask into the pocket of his mackinaw.

Sheriff Hayden, in the great bulk of his buffalo coat, walked toward their car, twisting his head down to see into the car's interior. His hands were in his pockets, and not just from the cold, Wesley guessed. His father often jammed his hands into his pockets when his temper was about to explode, when he couldn't be sure what he might do with his hands.

Frank was out of the car before his father came around to the side. "What did you think," Frank asked his father, "we wouldn't see you without the fire?"

Sheriff Hayden shook his head vigorously. "That is not the tone you want to be taking. No. No sir. Not after Len and I stood out here half the night, worrying and freezing our asses. No. You best start over."

"Hell, I half expected to see you coming our way. Every time I saw a pair of headlights I wondered if they were yours."

"We thought about it. Believe me, we talked about it." He looked in at Wesley. "How are you boys?"

"I think Lester's nose might be broke," Wesley answered. "It's swelled up pretty bad."

"Come on out of there, Lester. Let Len take a look."

As Tommy slid out of the car with Lester behind him, Mr. Hayden said, "Thomas Salter. If I didn't know you were a part of this, I would have guessed."

"When did you talk to Sheriff Cooke?" Frank asked his father.

"The first time? Late afternoon. Around 5:30, I reckon."

"They got more snow over that way," Wesley said, getting out of the car.

Both his father and brother looked at him but said nothing.

Len gently led Lester over toward the fire and hunched his tall frame down so he could look directly at Lester's nose.

"Tell me if I'm hurtin' you." After a moment of careful examination, Len said to Sheriff Hayden. "I don't know. Could be broke."

"Who had the pistol?" Sheriff Hayden asked the boys.

Neither Frank nor Wesley said anything but Lester spoke up. "It was Tommy's."

Sheriff Hayden nodded knowingly. "Where is it now?"

Frank answered, "Cooke confiscated all our guns. Rifles. Shotguns. Every one."

"He say anything about you getting them back?"

"We didn't even know he had 'em at first. They packed us up and we were down the road a good piece before we thought to look."

Len and Lester came back to the car. "That's too much," Len said. "Keeping the guns."

Sheriff Hayden shrugged. "His jurisdiction."

"I could see taking the pistol——" said Frank.

"——that was what got you in trouble. That more than anything. Boys waving a pistol around. That was stupid. Disrespectful and stupid."

"It was that Indian girl," Tommy said, his voice too loud for the still night. Then Tommy must have seen something in Sheriff Hayden's eyes——something glinting in the firelight——and he fell silent.

"Len, you want to take Lester and Tommy home?"

"Should I wake their folks?"

"Might just as well. With you telling the story maybe there'll be fewer versions floating around."

"How about a doctor for Lester?"

The sheriff gazed for a moment at Lester's swollen, discolored face. "No, let his folks decide about that."

Wesley watched Len lead Tommy and Lester to Len's car, and he felt again the separation from his two friends—his brother's friends—that he had felt when they walked out of that alley in McCoy, and he knew that he was privileged, his father's son, protected from some of the blows the world would inevitably offer.

His father stepped closer to the fire, took his hands from his pockets, and warmed them over the flames. "I suppose you two would like to get back home to your own beds."

"It wasn't us, Pop," Frank said. "It wasn't us that started any of it."

His father spit into the fire. "Doesn't matter. You're the only ones was Haydens. If it's just those two spreading trash around somebody else's territory, that's one thing. But you were there. And you had your name with you. You've got it everywhere you go. You can't take it off and put it on like a pair of boots. You're a Hayden. Like it or not. And you damn well better start thinking about what that means. Because you sure as hell don't seem to know now."

While his father was talking Wesley stepped away from the fire and looked back down the road in the direction from which they had come. It always surprised him, looking at snowy fields on a moonless night like this one, how briefly the snow's whiteness lasted in the dark. It seemed as though its pale glow should shine for miles, lighting up the path they had driven that night.

By now Frank was arguing with their father. "What were we supposed to do, goddammit. Why don't you tell us that?"

"If you don't know," his father said to Frank, "it's not going to do a damn bit of good for me to tell you. Now get back in your car and head for home. I'll be right behind you."

It took a few tries to get the Model T started, and while the boys cranked the car, their father scattered the fire and kicked snow on its remains. Soon they were heading west again. Once out of the firelight, Wesley could see into the distance. An occasional light from a farm or ranch had come on. It was time for predawn chores to begin.

"I wonder how long he's going to be on the rampage," Frank said.

Wesley didn't answer. He wondered if he was getting sick. He was so tired. His throat was dry and raspy, and he didn't think it was only from breathing in wood smoke. His jaw ached as if the cold had gotten deep into the joints. His head felt heavy and full and warm. He pulled off his glove and pressed the back of his hand to his forehead. He didn't know if he had a fever, but then his mother said your hand couldn't tell—it was always cooler than your forehead. If he told her he didn't feel well, she would hold him gently by the shoulders and put her lips, soft and warm, to his brow, the test she had used since he was a baby to determine if he had a fever. Wesley decided he wouldn't say anything to her.

Julian Hayden
(1899)

❀ ❀ ❀

J ULIAN Hayden came to Montana in 1898 with two vows: he was determined, first of all, to prove out his claim to a quarter section of land. To do that, according to the terms of the 1862 Homestead Act, he had to settle on the land in a more or less permanent dwelling (a sod house or railroad shack would qualify) and make improvements on the land for five years. Although Julian was only sixteen and homesteaders were supposed to be at least twenty-one, land was so plentiful in the region and the government wanted settlers so badly that homestead officers didn't check anyone's age too closely.

Julian Hayden's second vow was simpler in its terms but larger in its demand: he was determined to do a better job than his father of caring and providing for the family.

Julian brought his mother to Montana with him. She had a brother in Wolf Point who had promised to help them get started on their claim. As it turned out, his help consisted of giving them directions on how to build a tar-paper shack and advising them that if they paid more than twenty dollars for materials they were fools. Julian and his mother paid eighteen dollars and seventy-five cents.

Julian's sister Lorna, older by a year, stayed behind in Schofield, Iowa. High-strung and fearful, she was ill suited for life on the frontier. Before Julian and his mother left Iowa, he made certain that Lorna was comfortably situated by talking the Methodist minister, Reverend Willard West, into giving his sister a job. Reverend West had three young daughters and a sickly wife. In exchange for room, board, and a small monthly wage, Lorna would help care for the children. That was to be her only duty, Julian emphasized; he did not want his sister working like a slave in the minister's home. Reverend West agreed emphatically and reassured Julian; they had a hired girl to do housework—Lorna would simply watch the girls.

Once they were settled securely in Montana, Julian would send for his sister. But not before. There were depths of melancholy that Lorna constantly skirted, and Julian worried that the harshness of life on the plains might push her off the edge.

Julian also left his father behind, buried in the Schofield town cemetery. George Hayden had been killed outside his own barbershop and in full view of many of the local citizens. Including his own son.

A farmer was in town to buy supplies, and his horse, a big bay, was skittish from the moment they arrived. At every loud noise—a window slamming or a dog barking—the horse threatened to bolt. Finally, something happened—perhaps no more momentous than a white curtain suddenly blowing out through an open window—and the horse broke free and began to gallop down Main Street. Julian remembered thinking that the horse's hooves clattered so loudly on the cobblestones that it sounded as though a wagonload of logs was being dumped on the street.

Julian had been standing in the doorway of the harness shop where he worked, and as he followed the horse's progress he saw his father step into the street.

When Mr. Hayden finally saw the horse charging at him, he froze in indecision. Julian could tell his father didn't know what to do because he leaned first in one direction and then the other, as though he were feinting, trying to trick the horse into altering its path.

And for an instant the horse did slow, prancing sideways as though it wanted to avoid the man as much as the man wanted to avoid the horse. At the last moment, however, the horse could not make itself stop, and Julian's father—who finally decided which way to go— leaped in exactly the same direction as the horse veered.

The blow seemed no more than glancing, as though the horse were merely shouldering the man out of the way. But that was enough. Mr. Hayden, a small man, flew across the cobblestones as if propelled by an explosive.

Julian did not condemn his father for freezing in the horse's path. He could not, because when he saw his father struck, Julian behaved in exactly the same way. He could not make himself move from the doorway of the harness shop. From every direction people were running toward his father's body, but Julian simply stood there, the smell of the shop's leather filling his nostrils. Afterward, he would associate this smell with the horse's galloping escape, though he had no evidence that a piece of leather—a rein, a bridle, a tether—had failed.

When Julian finally reached his father's side, his father was already dead, as no doubt he had been from the instant his body struck the paving stones. There was not a mark on his body, a fact that later served to comfort his mother. She knew that her husband was not a good provider and never would be, but his good looks even in death pleased her. The doctor who signed the death certificate conjectured that perhaps Mr. Hayden had died of fright—that his heart had seized with fear when the horse bore down upon him. Julian doubted that diagnosis; after all, his father had jumped just before he was struck. He had simply jumped the wrong way.

Mr. Hayden did not leave his family much. He had insurance, but since he had fallen behind on the premiums the company did not pay off on the policy. His barbershop was not paid for. They did not own their home but rented from the widow of a prominent Schofield banker and politician. Worst of all, to Julian's way of thinking, his father had bequeathed him no trade or skill or even any tools with which a young man could make a living. He left behind a past—debts that had to be paid—but no future. Other than the few dollars Julian brought home from working after school in the harness shop, the family had no income. When Julian's uncle wrote that Montana was a place where someone could become a landowner with no other resource but a willingness to work hard, Julian persuaded his mother that this was the only opportunity that offered them a chance not simply to get by but eventually to prosper. When they left Iowa the only material reminders Julian took of his father were his barbers' scissors, a straight razor, and a strop. Everything else they sold or gave away, including a new wool suit. Julian had already outgrown his father's clothes.

Their shack measured twelve feet by fourteen feet. The exterior walls were covered with tar paper and the interior ones with newspapers. From an old sheepherder they bought a cookstove for preparing food and providing heat. Hay-stuffed bags served as mattresses on beds made from boards, poles, and ropes. They nailed cracker boxes and apple crates to the walls for shelves and used syrup pails and baking powder cans for food storage. Julian hadn't planned on having a wood floor their first year, but when someone made a remark about rattlesnakes coming up through holes in the dirt he changed his mind. They used their trunk for storage and as a table, and they bought two chairs at a farm auction. At the same auction they acquired a plow and a shaggy, scrawny pair of horses.

While he waited to pay for his purchases at the estate sale, Julian overheard a bandy-legged, leathery-skinned older man talking to a pair of young cowboys. "They brought this horse in with two brands," the old man said, "so I knew what I was in for. I saddled him and got on, and he did nothing but stand there. Still as a statue. Then, just when I was going to spur him, he threw his head straight back. Caught me right in the face. Broke my nose for me and knocked me on my ass. 'Somebody give me a quirt,' I says, and by God I brought that horse to his knees." If that was for breaking a man's nose, Julian wondered, what punishment would they have in Montana for a horse that killed a man?

During their first year on the homestead, Julian intended to plant wheat and potatoes while his mother raised a few chickens for eggs. Julian had a few other ideas for turning a dollar, but all those plans were short-term. As soon as he could manage it, he was going to start buying cattle. In Iowa, which had some of the richest soil in the country, plenty of farmers were still hard-pressed to get by, and Montana's soil was not Iowa's. Julian had paid attention as the train brought them across Minnesota and North Dakota and into Montana. Along the way the land's suitability for farming gradually gave out—the topsoil became thinner, drier, less fertile—and by the time they arrived in Mercer County it was obvious to him that this country was not meant for growing most crops. It was rangeland plain and simple, no matter who touted the benefits of dry farming or boasted about his latest yield of spring wheat. Besides, Julian didn't want to spend his life staring down at the dirt. The sky here was huge, and he wanted to be able to lift his sight and let it range as wide and far as he chose.

His mother wasn't much help with the work. She had often berated her husband for his shiftlessness, but the truth was, she had never been much of a worker herself. She spent most of the day sitting outside the shack, erect in her straightback chair, her hands folded serenely on her lap. She moved her head as though she was looking about, but her gaze was as blank as a blind person's. Julian was sure that if he asked her what she saw out there toward the horizon, she wouldn't be able to answer him. At night with the lamp off and both of them in bed, he could hear her crying softly. He knew her tears had nothing to do with grief over her husband's death. She hadn't cried in Iowa, so the conclusion was inescapable: she wept over this wind-swept place she had come to.

The letters from Lorna didn't help. Julian's sister wrote almost every day, brief letters that did little but complain. Julian suggested once that she save on postage by writing longer letters less frequently, but she wrote back and said that it helped her "to converse with her brother and dear mother every day, even if for a moment or two."

She mentioned her loneliness, though as Julian pointed out to his mother, Lorna remained in the same community she had lived in all her life; she had friends and relatives there, whereas they knew almost no one in Montana. She wrote that she missed them, but asserted in virtually every letter that life on the prairie would be too difficult for her.

And she complained of the work she had to do.

These grievances were muted and subtle at first. She said only that she was tired, the children were so lively, the hours of her days were so full she scarcely had a moment to herself. . . . Gradually she became more specific. She had dusted the pews in the church, lined up all the hymnals, and swept the steps before and after the service. She had helped out with the cooking in the West household. After this letter Julian wrote to Reverend West, politely reminding him that the agreement had been that his sister would care for the children; she was not to take the place of a hired girl. His sister's hardships did not lessen. Her hands hurt, she wrote, from polishing the family silver. She coughed all night because she had been beating rugs. Her knees ached from scrubbing floors.

This last charge appeared in a letter that arrived in the fall. The water barrel wore a thin membrane of frost that morning, and with each breath of wind a few snowflakes flew out of the north. When Julian finished his sister's letter, he said nothing to his mother. He did not care how hard he had to work on this miserable claim. No matter how brutal or dirty that work was, he was willing to do it because this was his land. But his sister was not going to wash another man's floors. Julian decided that he would have to return to Iowa to speak to the minister personally.

To get money for the trip back to Iowa, Julian sold his mother's chickens and hired himself out to every harvest crew that would have him. One day he finished working on one farm late in the afternoon and immediately walked to another field to begin work with another family. In spite of his own back-breaking labor, he never would have been able to earn his fare if not for his horses. He leased them out to two farmers who agreed to pay him in advance.

Before he left town Julian asked Len McAuley, a young man he had befriended, to look in on his mother while he was away. Len lived alone in a shack down by the Knife River, hunting, fishing, and trapping to get by. Julian had not only sought advice from Len, he had hired him a few times when the work on Julian's place was more than he could handle alone.

Len was grateful but more than that. He looked up to Julian and felt that simply being near Julian Hayden—who was confident, ambitious, self-assured—helped correct some of the drift and despair of Len's own life. Julian was more father than friend to Len McAuley, and any favor Julian asked Len would surely grant.

Julian bought a round-trip train ticket, specifying that arrival and departure times should be as close together as possible. If he couldn't take care of this matter quickly, he couldn't take care of it at all. Into a canvas duffel he put a few pieces of chicken, two pancakes rolled tight and smeared with apple butter, and some wild cherries, all wrapped in newspaper and a cloth napkin; he also packed a clean shirt, a handkerchief, and his father's straight razor. He told his mother that he was going to Helena, that it was necessary to have certain papers on file at the state capitol if you wanted to claim additional sections of land in the future. Julian's mother had no reason not to believe him.

He arrived in Iowa on a rainy Wednesday afternoon. In spite of the rain the day was warm, unseasonably so, and autumn's fallen leaves were plastered wetly to the sidewalks, streets, and curbstones. When Julian boarded the train in Montana, it was cold enough for him to wear his heavy mackinaw; the fact that he didn't need it now added to the feeling that he wasn't merely in another state but in another country. He couldn't remember Iowa being this warm so late in the year, but perhaps his life there was so far behind him he could no longer trust his memory of the place or its climate.

On Wednesday evenings Reverend West taught a Bible study class at the church that wouldn't conclude until around nine o'clock. Julian decided not to wait inside the depot but on a sheltered bench out on the platform. This trip was business; he didn't want anyone—not even old friends—asking him what he was doing in town or how long he would be staying. He was not planning even to see his sister; certainly he could resist the temptation to walk out front and look up and down Schofield's main street to see what might have changed since he moved away. He told himself that he didn't give a damn about this town; he was a Montanan now.

The rain stopped around dusk. As the evening cooled, mist rose from the streets. In the light around the street lamps, fog swirled so thickly that the entire town looked as though it was steaming from a recently extinguished fire.

St. Paul's Methodist Church was at the edge of town, a massive stone building surrounded by cornfields on every side but one. There the town cemetery, its tombstones and trees, crowded right up to the church. The rectory, a handsome white frame house built in recent years to accomodate Reverend West and his family, was on the other side of the cemetery, on the way into town. Julian chose to wait in the cemetery where he could see all the doors of the church as well as the path toward the rectory. He stood under a huge oak whose leafless branches steadily dripped rainwater. He was wearing his coat again, and to keep his mind occupied while he waited, he tried to see if he could feel any added weight on his shoulders as the wool of his coat absorbed those droplets of water. Then he gazed around him at the grave markers, straining his eyes in the darkness to make out what he could of the letters and numbers carved in the stone. The white limestone markers showed up better in the dark than the granite and marble tombstones, but limestone faded and eroded over time. In the oldest section of the cemetery the names and dates were barely readable. His father was buried near the only beech tree in the cemetery. Chiseled into the limestone was nothing more than his father's name and the dates of his birth and death.

Finally, through the side door closest to Reverend West's study, people began to leave the church and to walk toward town. As they passed the cemetery they spoke softly, but their voices carried perfectly through the damp, still air, and Julian could hear every word they said. A man said, "This weather—I tell you, it's a gift." A woman—this voice Julian believed he recognized—said, "You most certainly will not, I says to her. Not in this dwelling." He thought that was Mrs. Spark, a friend of his mother's, and he wondered if she was referring to her daughter Emily. Emily was Julian's age and they had been in school together. He remembered her as a plump, sullen girl who was so stupid that it pained him when she was called on to recite or read aloud in the classroom. Another passerby said, "Sometimes I envy those Catholics. I wish I could cross myself and be done with it."

Soon the last of the churchgoers walked by, and the night was quiet again. The minutes passed, and there was still no sign of Reverend West. Julian wondered if the minister could have gone out another door. No, he knew the church: there were the wide front doors and the small door in back; no other way in or out, and the fog was not thick enough to hide a man. Julian would simply have to wait patiently and keep watching.

The church's wide front doors opened. A man stood at the top of the steps, as if appraising the night, and then he opened his arms wide and held them out. He was no doubt doing nothing more than stretching his limbs and taking in a deep breath of the humid air, but to Julian it looked as though he was beckoning, calling forth something in the night. Then he descended the steps with a nimbleness surprising in so large a man.

Julian waited to make certain of the minister's route— yes, he would walk the same path that the other townspeople had taken—and then Julian left his post under the tree and moved swiftly to a point at the cemetery's edge where Reverend West was sure to pass. The day's rain helped Julian move quietly; the fallen leaves that would ordinarily crackle underfoot made no more noise than his footfall on the sodden turf of the graves.

Julian crouched beside a huge spirea bush, out of the minister's line of sight. This same spirea, Julian remembered, had been in bloom on the day of his father's burial, the bush so covered with white blossoms that it looked as though it carried a load of snow.

The moonless night, the fog, the bush, Reverend West's massive girth, which made it difficult for him to look down at his feet—all these things worked together to make it possible for Julian to reach out unnoticed just as the minister walked by. Julian tried to grab the minister's ankle. He missed and got more trouser leg than ankle but it was enough.

Julian pulled back as hard as he could and the minister went down with astonishing ease, pitching face forward onto the dirt path. He made no cry, but landed with the thump of a sandbag dropped from a great height. Julian wondered if the man had been frightened into unconsciousness.

He didn't wait to find out. In his hand he had his father's straight razor, the carefully stropped blade open and ready, and he scrambled up onto the minister's legs, keeping him pinned to the ground.

Julian wanted to draw blood but he didn't want to injure Reverend West seriously, so he tried to slice through just the fabric and the first layer of skin. As he slashed out across the minister's upper leg and buttocks, he realized how difficult it was to gauge the depth of the cut. The blade was so sharp that it could easily have gone right through muscle and artery down to bone. He should have practiced at home on something—a burlap bag of potatoes perhaps, or a cut of meat wrapped in an old shirt—so he could tell exactly how much force to exert.

Now Reverend West began to make noise, but Julian didn't believe the minister had yet realized that he was cut or bleeding. The reverend was simply gasping, taking in great honking gulps of air. He hadn't gotten over the shock of the attack; he probably didn't know whether he had been hurt or not.

Julian reached up and pushed Reverend West's head down into the dirt. "Don't try to get up," Julian said. "Don't or I'll hurt you bad. Worse." His hand slid to the side of the minister's head and caught his ear. I could slice it right off, Julian thought; I could cut it off and have it in my pocket before he even knew it was gone. And if he doesn't do as I say—

Reverend West made more gulping sounds. "I'll, I'll, I'll, I'll—" but Julian couldn't be sure if the minister was trying to speak or simply to breathe.

"Listen to me," Julian said. He knew he had a high soft voice and he tried to deepen it. "*Listen*. You've got Lorna doing more than she's supposed to. You got her scrubbing floors and washing clothes. She's to watch your children. Only that. You hear? Lorna Hayden isn't to do anything but watch those young ones."

Julian pushed himself up off the minister's great bulk. He felt he should do or say something else, but he couldn't think of what that might be. Did Reverend West know now that he had been cut? He must. Even if he didn't feel the pain—and maybe Julian had barely broken the skin—the blood's spreading warm wetness was sure to tell him, and a razor didn't have to cut deep to make blood flow like water. Unless the minister thought he had wet himself. At that thought Julian almost smiled. And then he knew what he wanted to say. "You don't have to look up. This here is Lorna's brother. Julian. You know me. Or you used to." He wished he could add a verse or phrase from the Bible to impress the minister, but none came to mind. Instead, Julian kicked Reverend West's ankle, and as he did, he noticed the type of shoe the minister wore. Hell, Bentrock's main street had gumbo thick enough to suck a thin little shoe like that right off a man's foot. "Remember my words," Julian said. The command struck him as having an almost Biblical sonority.

Julian ran back through the cemetery, stopping along the way to pick up his valise under the tree where he had left it. He folded up the razor and dropped it into the bag, wondering all the while if perhaps he shouldn't keep it in his pocket where he could get to it quickly if he needed to.

The whole business was over so quickly. How long had it lasted, start to finish? A minute? Thirty seconds? Reverend West hadn't said a word, unless you counted those stammering, gargled sounds. Yes, Julian had planned on using the razor on the minister, or at least he had been ready to, but he imagined that might happen during the course of argument, that when he could think of no appropriate retort to Reverend West's fancily worded excuses and explanations, *then* he'd pull out the blade and hold it under the preacher's nose. But once he'd attacked, it just seemed to make more sense to cut *first*. After carrying the razor all that distance, Julian felt he had to use it.

On his way out of the cemetery he thought he ran past the section where his father was buried, but he couldn't be sure. He was running swiftly, fog still hugged the ground, and so many of the graves looked alike.

Back at the depot he remained out on the platform, where he could keep watch in every direction and be ready to run if the police should come looking for him. When the night turned chill and a north wind blew away the clouds and mist to reveal a black starry sky, he wrapped himself tighter in his mackinaw and waited for his train.

The sky to the east had not lightened, but somewhere birds had begun to sing when Julian's train pulled into the Schofield station. He was the first to board, and once he was in his seat his relief was so complete that he fell asleep almost immediately. He had a dream that had troubled him since childhood.

In the dream he was standing by the shore of a lake or stream and reaching down for something—a coin or shining stone—just beneath the surface of the shallow water. When he put his hand down for the object, it moved away, as though his hand rippled the water just enough to carry the object out of reach. Or he put his hand into the water and suddenly the water was not shallow but deep, and the object was too far down for him even to touch, much less pick up. It had looked close only because of the clarity of the water. He knew in the dream that he wasn't going to be able to reach what he was after—he had known since early childhood—yet he couldn't keep from putting his hand in the water. He once told his mother about his dream, and she advised him to visit the bathroom before going to bed.

When he woke, the sun had warmed the side of his face that had been resting against the train's window. Outside he saw what he believed to be the planted fields and gentle hills of Minnesota, and he knew he was safe.

✳

Lorna Hayden never joined her mother and brother in Montana, but she did not work long for the West family. A young man came to the house to tune the West's piano, and within a month he and Lorna were married. They made their home in Des Moines, where his father owned a music store, a business made prosperous by selling and renting band instruments to Iowa schools. Lorna and her husband did not visit Montana until they had been married for almost ten years and had three children.

Julian's mother moved into Bentrock, the nearest town, after their first winter, and she never returned to live on the homestead. Julian worked even harder, not only to keep the farm going but to make certain that his mother could live comfortably in town.

For the rest of her life, scarcely a month went by when Julian's mother did not gratefully lift to her lips her son's hands—hands once calloused from farm and ranch work but softened when Julian himself moved to town to buy and sell real estate and eventually to become his county's Clerk of Court and finally its sheriff. She would kiss the palm of each of her son's hands and say, "You take such good care of me. These hands can do anything."

Enid Garling
(1906)

❀ ❀ ❀

O<small>N THE</small> Saturday before Palm Sunday, the day she was to marry Julian Hayden, Enid Garling had one fervent wish: she hoped that her father, Bertram Garling, would not appear at the church. If he did, it would be for one reason and one reason only: to stop the wedding and take Enid home with him. And if her father came, Julian Hayden would surely try to stop him any way he could.

Enid left her home in Wild Rose, North Dakota, only two days before the wedding. She could leave because her father was temporarily living in Washington state with his brother, providing food for the men working in the lumber camps. Her father didn't assist in the actual preparation of the food—his brother and sister-in-law did that—but he helped purchase the supplies, hunted and fished, and drove the chuck wagon from camp to camp. Once Enid decided to leave, she had to get out quickly; her father might return at any time when it became clear that this venture, like so many others, would not make him a wealthy man. And when he came back, he would rely on Enid to tell him where they should next try to make their fortune.

Bertram Garling believed that his only daughter had the power to see the future, a belief he had held since an incident that occurred when Enid was four years old.

They lived in Wisconsin then, or, more precisely, they had just moved to the state. Mr. Garling had been working in the family dairy in Rockford, Illinois, since he was a boy, and he decided he didn't want to spend his life rising before dawn just to sit with his head leaning against one cow after another. He had an opportunity to try running a small cheese factory, so he moved with his family to Prescott, Wisconsin. When they first pulled up to their rented house, Enid went to the back door, took one look inside the house's tiny kitchen, screamed hysterically, and backed away from the open door. Enid's mother picked up her daughter to carry her into the family's new home.

Mr. Garling, a superstitious man, was quick to excuse any behavior on the part of his beloved daughter, and he said, "Wait! She sees something! Something has frightened her!"

"There's nothing in there," Enid's mother said. Enid's brother, Hiram, older by three years, was already in the house, and he confirmed his mother's assessment. "It's empty all right!"

"Nothing we can see," Mr. Garling said, "but the child might have powers of sight that we lack."

Mrs. Garling scoffed. Less than four months later, however, it was Hiram who was carried into the kitchen, and his dead body was laid on the kitchen table. He had drowned in a neighbor's cistern. Mr. Garling was convinced that on their first day in Wisconsin, Enid had had a vision of her brother dead in the house. From that day on he would make no decision about the family without first consulting his daughter to determine whether she had a vision about their future.

And though she had no memory of what frightened her that day, Enid *did* see things. She could close her eyes at any time, day or night, and within minutes a form or shape would emerge from the darkness. The image never lasted long. She could seldom catch more than a glimpse of it, as if she were looking from the window of a fast-moving train. The import of these visions was even hazier. It was up to her father to interpret exactly what they meant and what actions should be taken on the basis of what Enid saw. In fact, her father played such an important role in this process that by the time Enid was in her early teens she wondered if she ever saw anything on her own or if she merely reproduced what her father implanted.

Perhaps the gift was not hers but her father's—he could make people see something that wasn't there. Nevertheless, every plan he undertook, every move the family made—to Minnesota to try wheat farming, to South Dakota to try gold mining, to Wyoming to try marketing a friend's newly invented windmill pump, or to North Dakota to try capturing and selling wild horses—came only after Enid had a vision— of a patch of green grass, of water running down a rocky slope, of a man and woman standing in the shadow of a stone tower. Enid was secretly pleased whenever her father had a plan that required him to leave his family for any length of time, because it meant that the swarm of whirling images in her brain would temporarily subside.

Enid's mother tried to find ways to free Enid from her father's domination and to allow her the life that other girls had.

Mrs. Garling made certain that her daughter was always enrolled in school, even though Enid was so shy that any occasion requiring her to leave the house caused her so much distress she became physically ill. Mrs. Garling was not deterred; if she had to walk her weeping daughter to the schoolhouse, then so be it. Since Enid had difficulty making friends, her mother signed her up for membership in clubs and organizations. Mrs. Garling made it a point to befriend women who had daughters near Enid's age. Yet her efforts did little to transform Enid from the strange, fearful, reclusive child she had been since infancy. As part of her efforts on Enid's behalf, Mrs. Garling signed Enid up for piano and singing lessons, and it became apparent that Enid had gifts of a more conventional nature than vague visions of the future.

She took to the piano instantly, and could play almost any tune by ear. She had as well a lovely, delicate soprano voice, as pure and effortless as rushing water. Whenever they moved into a new community, Mrs. Garling advertised her daughter's talents, and Enid was often asked to perform at civic, school, and church functions.

It was at one of those affairs, the weekly Friday night Wild Rose Dance Club meeting, that Julian Hayden first saw Enid Garling and heard her sing. This was August 1905 and Julian and Len McAuley had come from Montana to buy cattle from a North Dakota rancher.

The night was hot and damp, and the dance club was meeting, as it did throughout the summer, under a large canvas tent staked out in the school yard. A platform of planks was laid for dancing, and benches were set up in the tent and in the yard for rest and refreshment. During the band's intermission, Enid Garling, accompanying herself on the piano, entertained the crowd. Julian heard her sing "In the Gloaming."

Julian Hayden was not the first man to be attracted to Enid Garling. She had pale, luminous skin, large brown eyes, finely sculpted features, and a trim figure. She wore her luxurious dark brown hair swept up into a pompadour held in place with tortoiseshell combs. She accentuated the grace of her long neck with high-collared blouses and high-necked dresses.

But men drawn to Enid Garling's beauty always backed away. They saw that agitation shimmered in the very air around her, that she trembled her way through the most ordinary exchange of small talk, that her eyelids fluttered as though she were always on the verge of fainting.

And here was another suitor. A tall, sunburnt, wide-shouldered cowboy who was probably Enid's age but who tried to look older by sporting a dark, drooping moustache. He didn't say a word but leaned on the piano and listened, never taking his eyes from her, never ceasing his smile.

His presence made it difficult for her to sing. She tried to concentrate on the lyrics but then she worried that he might believe she was singing those words especially for him. She stopped singing altogether and simply played the piano, but he stayed where he was. When the song was finished, he applauded her so loudly that his hands clapping together sounded like gunshots. She wanted to cover her ears but instead merely bowed her head. Then he said something she had never heard said about her singing or playing: "Civilizing. Very civilizing." And he walked away.

In the next few months Enid came to understand what Julian Hayden meant by his remark. He came to Wild Rose at every opportunity, sometimes arriving in the middle of the night and sleeping in his wagon in their yard. Enid wondered whether she finally weakened in her resistance to his affection because he so often simply appeared—there, under the willow tree when she looked out her bedroom window; there, in front of the mercantile when she exited the store; there, alongside the railroad tracks where Enid walked on her way to the post office or butcher shop—like a figure in one of her visions. From the very first time he came to call, Julian Hayden made his intentions clear: he wanted Enid to marry him, to marry him and return with him to his home near Bentrock, Montana. There, her delicacy, her fine manners, her music would help to soften and civilize that rough, wild region. She would give it beauty. He repeated this argument so often that she began to wonder if he wanted her for his state's sake or his own.

She learned that he was indeed very close to her age— twenty-four. In fact, he was seven months younger than she. He owned a small ranch that he was working hard to enlarge. His father was no longer alive, but he supported his mother, who lived in a rented room in Bentrock; life on the ranch was too hard for her. He was determined, ambitious, confident— so many things she was not. And he was persistent.

He loved to talk about horses and his skill in breaking them. From a boy new to Montana who couldn't even sit on a horse correctly he had become, in his opinion, the best bronco buster in his part of the state. Life had no satisfaction, he said, like getting a horse to walk how and when you wanted him to walk. His secret, as he told Enid many times, was discovering how a horse thinks. "Now a horse, he's got no sense of time," Julian would say. "It doesn't mean anything to him that you've been climbing up on him for four or five hours. He doesn't know that by now he's supposed to be getting the idea that you're in charge. He doesn't care if it's ten o'clock or two o'clock. All he knows is one thing: he's either got the energy to rear up and throw you off or he doesn't. Time makes people give up. They say, 'I guess I won't be riding that horse. I've been at it for hours and he still hasn't settled down.' But there's only one thing to do. Get back on. And keep getting back on. Plenty of fellows can stay in the saddle longer than I can, but nobody's better at dusting himself off and getting back on. Nobody. Like that horse, I just forget about what time it is, and I keep at him. And I haven't come across a horse yet that won't give up before I do." He would talk about saddles and one-ear bridles and Spanish bits, about how to keep a horse from fighting the reins all day, how to cinch him so he'll carry you fifty miles if need be, how to make sure you train a cow horse to be ground tied.

But Enid couldn't keep from her mind what he said about breaking horses. She had the uneasy feeling that he was practicing the same technique on her, that she could put him off for any number of days, weeks, months, years, and Julian Hayden would keep coming back.

He had her mother's help. As if she had her own visions of the future, Mrs. Garling told her daughter over and over what her life would be like if she rejected this young man's suit.

107

Soon her father would return, but then he would be off again—up to Saskatchewan to work in an oil field, or down to Medora to be a partner in a slaughterhouse, or out to the Judith Mountains to raise sheep, or back to Wisconsin to run freight on the river. He'd always have another scheme, and he'd badger Enid until she told him what he wanted to hear— that this time he couldn't miss; this time he'd become a success. If Enid didn't take this opportunity to get out, she'd end up traipsing around the country with her momma and daddy forever, and the closest she would come to pleasure in this life would be singing and playing the piano at other women's weddings. Give yourself a chance, Mrs. Garling said to her daughter; give yourself a chance to know and love a man, to settle down and to know and love a place.

When Enid Garling told Julian Hayden she would marry him, he gave no sign of rejoicing. He didn't laugh or weep with happiness. He didn't throw his hat in the air or sweep Enid into his arms as she hoped he might. He said simply and solemnly, "This is right."

Enid did not reveal to Julian that her father believed she was capable of prophetic visions, but she did tell him that her father was certain to oppose the marriage. Her father had pampered her, she said, and he would not want her living on a ranch in Montana. He had always tried to protect his daughter, and he would not want her living in a region that he thought rough, crude, and untamed.

She hoped that when she told Julian about her father, Julian would say, "Well, from now on *I'll* be the one protecting you."

He did not. He threw his head back and laughed. Then he said, "Your father's a smart man. He's absolutely right. It's the Wild West!" Then he looked at her with an expression she hadn't seen before. He squinted his eyes as though he were trying to make out her features in a darkened room. "He'll play hell trying to take you away from me."

He was so sure of himself that she searched for something to say that would take him down a notch. "Don't underestimate Papa. Ask my mother. She'll tell you."

He only laughed again.

Julian Hayden brought Enid to Montana two days before the wedding. He wanted to show her his ranch and the town of Bentrock, and he wanted her to meet his mother.

He had never represented his ranch to her as anything but a hardscrabble spread, so Enid was not shocked or disappointed to see it. The ranch lay in a little valley—hardly a valley at all—a wrinkle, a fold in the earth, marked white by an alkali bed. Running through the valley was a stream whose span Enid could step across and whose flow she could outcrawl. There was a horse barn and corral, and an open cattle shed. There was a shack that had been the original building on the homestead, and growing out from that tiny shack was the beginning of a new two-story house. The house was framed up, and the first floor was finished, but the second floor was nothing but studs and rafters. A ranch wagon and two buggies cluttered the yard, and harness and tack hung from the barn wall and corral posts. The outhouse stood on a small rise about sixty feet from the house's back door. Julian said that since a blizzard two winters ago he kept a rope strung between the house and the privy, so you could be sure of finding your way out and back again. None of the buildings was painted, and their wood had weathered to a windburned gray. Vegetation consisted of a few patches of coarse grass in front of the house, and a stand of five or six spindly cottonwoods growing along the banks of the tiny creek. Otherwise there was nothing but rocks, sandy soil, and sagebrush. Yet Julian pointed to every broken wagon wheel and rusting barrel ring with such pride that Enid felt she must try hard to match his enthusiasm for what would be her new home. Before they left for Bentrock he waved his hand around the ranch and said, "And if you give me enough sons, we can make this place into something that will have them all whistling with envy."

Enough sons, Enid wondered. How many sons would be enough?

Julian's mother lived in a cramped apartment above a bakery in Bentrock. The aroma of baking bread rose from the ovens below and filled the three tiny rooms day and night with a heavy, warm, yeasty smell that settled on your tongue as well as in your nostrils. Enid would stay there with Mrs.

Hayden until the wedding, an arrangement that Enid thought would give her an opportunity to find out more about her husband-to-be. Who would know him better than his mother? But Mrs. Hayden was not at all what Enid had expected.

She was a remote, somber woman who had none of her son's vitality or good humor. She dressed in black and Enid's first impression was of a woman in mourning. She spent most of her time sitting in a rocking chair staring down at the street below. To virtually every question Enid put to her, whether about Julian or the community or herself, Mrs. Hayden simply turned a squinted eye in Enid's direction and offered a brief, cryptic answer. Enid asked her if she liked Montana, and Mrs. Hayden said, "This is my home." Enid suggested that their first days on the homestead must have been very difficult, and Mrs. Hayden said, "Harder than some. Not all." Enid tried to find out what the people of Bentrock were like, and Mrs. Hayden pointed out the window and said, "They're out there. Not much point in me telling you." And when Enid said that Julian seemed an ambitious man who was certain to go far, Mrs. Hayden clacked her teeth a few times before replying, "Not far from his mother, that's sure."

Enid had hoped to tell Mrs. Hayden something of her own life, of the many places she had lived, of the occupations her father had tried, of her concerns about living a settled life, but since Julian's mother asked her no questions, Enid felt uncomfortable volunteering information. Instead Enid thought she might win Mrs. Hayden's favor by working around the apartment, by dusting the furniture, sweeping the carpet, and by scouring the kitchen and bathroom fixtures. Mrs. Hayden

111

didn't acknowledge Enid's efforts but continued rocking in her chair while Enid worked.

Strangest of all were the meals Julian's mother prepared for Enid and herself. Mrs. Hayden served oatmeal for breakfast, lunch, and dinner, but supplemented the mush at noon with sliced stale bread (no butter or jam to moisten it), and at the evening meal she fried a few slices of side pork. Buttermilk was the drink at every meal. Obviously Mrs. Hayden saw nothing unusual about this fare, for she did not apologize nor comment on it. She set the portions before Enid and took the dishes away when they were empty.

Mrs. Hayden retired early and for that Enid was grateful. As soon as she heard her snores, Enid rose from her own bed—she was to sleep on the hard horsehair couch—and took up Mrs. Hayden's post by the window. What did she find to look at all day? What would the night disclose?

Enid directed her gaze first in one direction and then the other. A U.S. Land Office. The Merland Brothers General Store—Dry Goods and Groceries. The Stockman's Bank of Montana with its stone eagle above the double doors and in its upper windows a sign advertising Rasmussen and Son, Attorneys at Law and Notary Public. Whirtle's Confectionary. The Austin House Hotel. The Royal Theater. The Silver Dollar Bar and Billiards. If she leaned out the window she might be able to see the cupola of the courthouse where she and Julian were issued their marriage license, and beyond the courthouse's dome the spire of the church where she would be married.

Bentrock resembled other towns she had lived in or near

all her life. The wooden walkways. The dusty streets. The gaslights. The dogs barking back and forth in the distance. She was certain that after only a few moments at the window she could close her eyes and in her mind reproduce every business, every store, every gilt-painted sign in every darkened window.

When she heard footsteps, she opened her eyes. A man was leaving the bar and his boots beat a slow rhythm on the sidewalk's planks. The night was so still Enid could close her eyes again and plot his progress by ear. She tapped her finger on the windowsill in time with his steps. The rhythm reminded her of a song, and she softly hummed its melody.

She became suddenly self-conscious, and this time when she opened her eyes she saw someone she was certain hadn't been there before.

Directly across from her, sitting on a barrel in front of Merland Brothers, was an Indian. The evening was cool, and he was wrapped in a blanket so mottled it could have been a dirty, moth-eaten patchwork of fabric or fur. He was hatless and his long hair hung in lanky strands, partially covering his face. Nevertheless, Enid could see that he was old, and by the way he wavered back and forth on the barrel she concluded that he was either drunk or fighting to stay awake. While she watched him, his face turned upward and he seemed to be staring at her. His gaze was so blank she wondered if he saw her. Was he in a trance? Was he looking past her, at something in the night sky that commanded his attention?

Enid slipped from the window and back to her bed on the couch. She lay awake for a long time, fighting the impulse to go to the window again to see if the Indian was still out there. At some point she thought she could feel that he was no longer there, and she soon fell asleep.

In one of her dreams she was at the window again, but she did not look out on a street deserted and dark but lit by high noon's sunlight. And she was not looking for an old Indian sitting on a barrel but for her father, who was, she was certain, about to appear on Bentrock's Main Street.

While she watched he actually appeared, charging down from the east in a whirlwind of dust. He drove up and down the street in a rickety buckboard pulled by an entire herd of animals—cows, horses, sheep, deer, antelope. Even in the dream she thought she would have to ask her father how he managed to hitch so many animals of so many kinds to a wagon. Julian would want to know, she thought; this information would be useful for her husband to have for his ranch. Then she realized that the wagon and team were her father's latest scheme: he had invented a way to make these animals work together and pull a wagon. At last, she thought, he had hit upon something that might make him rich.

She was sure that her father had come for her, yet he showed no sign that he was looking for her or even that he knew she was in town. He didn't stop in front of the bakery and climb the narrow stairs to the apartment. He didn't stand on the seat of his buckboard and bellow her name until she answered. He didn't stop anyone on the street and demand his daughter's whereabouts or ask where he could find the man who was going to marry her. Soon Enid realized that he wasn't there for her at all; he was simply advertising his new invention—this team of animals and the elaborate system of ropes, harnesses, webs, and pulleys by which he kept them all together. Then this dream flowed into the next. A driverless motorcar drove down Main Street, and her father and his team weren't there at all. There was only the motorcar, spinning in a tight circle as if it were a horse tethered to a snubbing post, and while it churned up a cloud of choking dust, Enid forgot about her father and wondered—could a motorcar actually do that?

Enid was surprised to find that the wedding would not be held in the church, but in the yard between the church and the cemetery. Julian had made this arrangement because the church was small and he wanted as many people as possible to attend the ceremony, and because he had once quarreled with a minister (not the one who would marry them), and from that day on he stayed out of churches if possible.

An outdoor wedding suited Enid. The weather was pleasant enough—in fact very warm for April—when it could as easily have been snowing. She remembered going to Easter services, one of the few occasions when Enid herself attended church, just the previous year and having to step through snow to enter the church. Today, only the wind marred the day's beauty. It blew hot and hard from the south. Since that part of Montana had not had much snow the past winter and since the spring had been dry, the wind was able to raise enough dust to dim the day's sunlight and to deposit a thin layer of silt on every unmoving surface. And when a hard gust came, you needed to turn your head to keep the bits of blowing sand and grit from your eyes. Enid's mother had bought Enid a new pancake hat for the wedding, but when Enid saw the wind's force she put the hat back in its box.

Being outside also allowed Enid to watch for her father's approach. Her mother had stayed behind in Wild Rose in case her father returned. She would explain to him that Enid was already gone, married to a Montana rancher, and would try to convince him to accept the situation. But Enid knew her father and his ability to make Mrs. Garling do what he wished. He would not use force on Enid's mother, and he wouldn't threaten her. But he had a power that made it seem as though natural forces were on his side—as though the rocks and the rivers wanted you to submit to his will—and Enid's mother might not be able to resist telling him what was happening in Bentrock on this day. Enid didn't expect him to show up, but she knew she would be foolish not to be on the lookout for him. To any prayer she said on her wedding day, she would silently add, And please, God, don't let my father come.

On the way to the church, Enid tried to explain to Julian what it might mean if her father came. "I'm afraid," she said. "What if my father comes?"

Julian was in such high spirits he could not take any warning seriously. "If he comes," he said and laughed, "he comes! Everyone's welcome here today."

"You don't understand. He might make trouble."

"Wait until you see Ernie Fergusson get into the jug. You'll see some trouble!"

She almost told him, I had a dream. I saw my father in the dream. But she stopped herself.

The wedding was scheduled for early afternoon, and the number of people who came astonished Enid. Not only was a sizable portion of the Bentrock population there, but farmers, ranchers, and sheepherders from the surrounding countryside as well. She knew they came primarily for the free food and drink, but the crowd pleased her anyway. They came because Julian invited them. Surely they must like and respect him. And though they didn't know her—and she didn't know them—she felt, nonetheless, that on this day they were compatriots. She didn't dare think of herself as a Montanan yet, but perhaps today she would be wedded to the region as well as to Julian Hayden.

Julian pulled into a small grove of trees. The churchyard was already filled with other buggies, with farm wagons, with spirited saddle horses, and with shaggy, heavy workhorses. Enid was certain that Julian's high-stepping blacks were the best-looking horses of the group.

Next to the church was a lectern covered with a white cloth held in place by a rock. Not far from this makeshift altar were the tables laden with food and drink. As Julian and Enid came closer, she saw the pans of fried chicken, the platters of steaks and ribs, the bowls of beans, the stacks of fresh-baked bread, the crocks of fresh-churned butter, and the pies cut from their tins and stacked three and four high. To drink there were gallons of milk and pitchers of home-brewed beer and jugs and bottles of whiskey. An older man turned the crank on an ice cream freezer while a small group of children pushed close to see his progress. The crowd cheered Julian and Enid as they approached, and one man, a tall, ruddy-faced rancher with a patch over one eye, said, "Jules, let's hurry up and get you hitched so we can get to the grub!"

"We'll take care of that directly, but before anyone ties on the feedbag you're all going to hear my new missus sing and play the piano."

That was when Enid noticed the piano and stool set up under a large oak tree. She had sung at weddings before, but at her own? A woman was not supposed to sing at her own wedding! And this wind would tear the words to any song right out of her mouth before anyone could hear her. She started to protest, but Julian said, "That's what they came for. To hear you." As she looked around at the people assembled in the churchyard, she had difficulty believing that anyone cared whether she sang or not.

The briefest wedding Enid ever witnessed was her own. The minister pronounced them man and wife after so few words that she wondered if he hadn't omitted an essential part of the ceremony. Before he kissed her, Julian made a great show of brushing his moustaches out of the way.

Then it was over. She was no longer Enid Garling but Enid Hayden. Everyone cheered, and amid the shouted congratulations and the handshakes and the backslaps, Enid was ushered to the piano, where Julian instructed her to play.

"What should I play?" she asked.

"You're the musician. You pick something."

She touched his hand. "What's your favorite song?"

He began to back away, moving toward the tables, where

his friends waited to toast his marriage. "Anything," he said. "Anything you play is my favorite."

She had a repertoire of songs that she was often requested to play and sing at weddings, but none of these would be appropriate for the bride herself to sing. Finally she settled on a Stephen Foster song, but since the piano was set up so that Enid's back was turned to the crowd, she couldn't be sure anyone listened to her. When she finished her song she heard no applause or acknowledgment of any kind.

While she waited and tried to think of another song, an old man, so thin Enid wondered if a gust of wind might blow him off his feet, approached her. He leaned on the piano and asked, "Do you know 'Lorena'?" His voice was amazingly deep and strong for a man who looked so frail.

She nodded.

"By God, I'd love to hear that again. I first heard it during the war. A young soldier from Pennsylvania used to sing it. Never heard anything so beautiful."

Enid was sure he meant the Civil War, but she didn't question him. She just began to play and sing, and the old man closed his eyes and gently tapped the top of the piano with his long, knotted fingers. His lips moved while she sang, but she couldn't be sure if any sound escaped.

Before she could finish the song, Julian returned. He had taken off his suit jacket, his vest, his tie, and his collar. He had bought a new collar for the occasion, and Enid could see that it had been too tight; a red rim, as fine as a pencil line, circled his neck. He had a thick black cigar jammed awkwardly in the corner of his mouth, and when he spoke he raised his voice to get the words past the cigar. "Come here," he said. "You got to see someone."

The muscles in her legs contracted into icy bands, and she couldn't get up. She was certain Julian meant that her father was there. He hadn't said she had to *meet* someone but *see* someone—that must mean it was someone she already knew. Who else could it be?

"Come on," Julian repeated, and he put his hand around her upper arm and made to lift her from the stool. His hand was almost large enough to encircle her arm, and she could feel the fabric bunch and twist against her skin. It was a new blouse. Enid feared that if Julian's hand was dirty, the bishop sleeve would bear his handprint and she would not be able to wash it out. In the months they had known each other he had touched her many times and in many ways, but he had never handled her so roughly. She couldn't be sure—was she making a judgment about marriage and her new husband or was she simply preparing herself to go back to Wild Rose with her father?

She stumbled to her feet and tried to keep up with him, though her long skirt made it difficult to match his long strides.

"I want you to look over these Roosian girls," Julian said. He pointed toward three young women standing by the food table. They were a few years younger than Enid—late teens, she figured—and they were dressed in new or freshly laundered shirtwaists (although they were not wearing corsets), yet they seemed uncomfortable in their clothing. One of the young women had taken off her shoes and stockings and her

120

bare feet were darkened with dirt. All three were considerably shorter than Enid, and the barefoot girl was quite plump. She also had breasts larger than any Enid had ever seen.

"You get to know them," Julian instructed Enid. "Pick one you like. She'll be your hired girl."

"Mine?"

"You didn't think I'd have you breaking those piano fingers on ranch work, did you?"

Enid looked at the girls' hands. They didn't seem so different from hers. "I can work," she said. "I want to."

"Oh, there'll be work aplenty. Don't you worry. But I don't want you scrubbin' floors or stringin' wire."

Enid had scrubbed floors before, but she wasn't sure she knew what he meant by "stringing wire." She imagined it had to do with putting up barbed wire fences. One of these girls would do that work?

Julian left her side again. "Some of us are getting a baseball game going. Why don't you have something to eat and then come over and watch the game?"

They had originally planned to leave the wedding early so they could travel to Williston, North Dakota, and spend the night in a hotel, an arrangement that especially pleased Enid because it meant that if her father did come, they might already be gone.

"I thought we were leaving before two," she said.

"I can't disappoint these fellows. They want me to pitch for them. They want me to use my drop ball on those hitters from over Delton way." Delton was a small town in an adjoining county.

121

Before Enid could say another word, Julian was gone, and when he rejoined his friends, she heard them cheer his return.

She turned back to the three girls and smiled at them. She had no idea what to say to them—had Julian already spoken to them about working on their ranch? Did they know Enid would be their employer?

Enid pointed to the platter still stacked high with wedges of pie. "Are any of those pies of your preparation?" she asked.

The heavy-breasted barefoot girl smiled at Enid but when she spoke it was in a foreign tongue, a garble of clicking consonants and little explosions of air that were almost like grunts. Although she never took her eyes from Enid, obviously what she said was for the benefit of her friends. They tried to suppress their laughter, but they could not hold back. Finally all three of them turned their backs to Enid so they could giggle and chatter in their own language. Enid walked away.

She found the baseball game being played in a field right below the church's cemetery. She sat down in the grass on a gentle rise where she could watch Julian and the other players.

She had never seen baseball before, and the game was absolutely incomprehensible to her. She knew the players were supposed to be arranged in teams, but she couldn't tell who played with whom. Some players threw the ball, some tried to hit it, some tried to catch it—and others ran in different directions while all this was going on. She could not even tell what the game's object was, what indicated winning and losing. On a makeshift bench alongside the playing field the players had placed pitchers of beer, and men drank from them at regular intervals. Enid didn't know if the drinking was part of the game or not. Was there a certain performance that was rewarded with a draught of beer?

Others came to watch the game too, but they crowded around the field, while Enid stayed where she was; she didn't know what the game's boundaries were, and she did not want to place herself where she might be in the way. The spectators cheered certain actions, but again, since Enid did not know which players or teams the observers favored, their applause and shouts of encouragement were as baffling to her as the game itself.

She did note that Julian was often at the center of the game's action and that he handled the ball as often as anyone. Did he want everyone to hit the ball or only certain players? He frequently shouted instructions to other players. Was that part of his duty on the field?

The afternoon wore on. Occasionally someone looked back at Enid sitting alone on the hill, but no one approached her or invited her to join them. Her boredom grew to the point where she became drowsy, and she thought of lying back on the grass and going to sleep. Yet she worried that if she closed her eyes, that would be the moment her father would appear.

The game finally ended, not, apparently, because a team won but because they lost the ball. A player hit it into a slough directly across from Enid, and although every player and many of the spectators walked up and down the length of the ditch, stamping down the tall grass and pushing aside the clumps of sage and thistle, no one found the ball. After the search there was a discussion about going after another ball, but no one knew where another could be obtained. Did no one bring his own? Did no store sell them? The players, sweat- and dirt-stained, finally drifted off the field, and the crowd followed them.

Enid stood and waved her handkerchief to Julian, and after a long moment he acknowledged her with a wave of his own, but he continued to walk back to the churchyard with the rest of the ball players.

The end of the game seemed to signify the end of the wedding celebration as well. When Enid returned from her post on the hillside, she saw that the tables of food were being taken down, the leftovers being wrapped and dispersed among the guests, and people were heading toward their horses and buggies. She didn't see Julian anywhere, but she hoped they could leave soon.

Then she saw him, coming from behind the church with his friend Len McAuley. Julian had his coat and tie back on, and she could tell from his slicked-back hair and glistening skin that he had washed up.

"Do you want to take any of that grub?" Julian asked her.

She shrugged, unsure of the correct response.

"One of those pies maybe?"

"If you like."

"I'm not much of a pie eater."

Enid smiled shyly. "I'm not either."

"Let's head out then." He took her arm—gently this time—and led her toward the buggy.

Len called out after them, "We'll take care of it here."

It was not until they were seated in the buggy and rolling out of the churchyard that Julian said, "You don't have to worry about your father showing up. Len's been watching. And he'll make sure no one's on our trail."

Enid nodded. Apparently Julian had taken her warnings more seriously than she had thought.

The church was on the west side of town, and they were traveling east, so they had to drive right through Bentrock. As they left town, heading east toward Williston, they came to a narrow bridge over the Knife River. The river was not wide or deep, but cottonwoods grew thickly along and up the bank, so it seemed, as they approached the bridge, that they were about to enter a tunnel. Here, just before the bridge's planks, Enid's father stood. When she saw him she wanted to weep. He was wearing a dark suit, and he never wore a suit. He had dressed for her wedding.

She tugged on Julian's sleeve. "Don't stop," she said. "You don't have to stop."

"That's him?" Julian asked.

"Yes," she answered.

Julian began to rein in the horses, and Mr. Garling took that opportunity to step into the road.

Julian pulled back hard on the reins. "Mister," he said to Enid's father, "that's how my own father got himself killed. Stepped right into a horse's path."

Mr. Garling stepped to the side and loosely gripped the

harness trace. "Oh, not these animals. They don't want to muddy their feet on the likes of me."

"Go," Enid whispered to her husband. "Just go."

"We've got a ways to travel," Julian said to Mr. Garling.

Her father said, "Enid, are you going to introduce me to the gentleman there by your side?"

She turned her head so she was speaking into the coarse weave of Julian's suit coat. "This is my father."

"And I take it," Mr. Garling said, "that this dashing gentleman is the groom."

"Julian Hayden," Enid's husband said.

"I'm familiar with the name. That's a name people speak with respect."

"Now it's her name too," Julian said.

Her father kept his hand on the trace and walked toward the buggy. "You're traveling east."

"That's right."

"I thought you might be taking her back to North Dakota. Back to Wild Rose. I thought your conscience might have gotten the better of you."

Julian didn't say anything.

"I thought you might be bringing her back to her mama and her papa. Seeing as how we have not blessed this union. A man who marries a little girl away from her folks like that—well, sooner or later his conscience is bound to bother him."

As her father spoke, Enid could feel his power increasing. It was as if he were casting a spell, enchanting them, and while it was happening they couldn't stop him. And when he was finished, it would be too late. As it was for her already—she knew she should say something to refute what her father said, but if she opened her mouth no words would come out.

Julian didn't say anything either, though Enid knew that what her father said certainly enraged her husband. Julian reached down to the floor of the buggy and picked up the cigar box that he always kept there. Enid had seen once before what was in the box. Every time Julian killed a rattlesnake he cut off its rattles and saved them in that box. She hated the sight of them, and Julian often teased her with the box, threatening to open it in her presence.

He rested the box carefully on his lap and with both hands lifted the lid. He was moving so slowly, so deliberately, that Enid thought for an instant that this time he had a live rattlesnake in the box.

Then, in a motion almost quicker than Enid's eye could follow, Julian brought the pistol out of the box and pointed it at her father.

Everything was still again. Julian held his arm straight out, the small chrome-plated pistol aimed right at her father's chest. Her father's hand tightened around the harness leather. The horses, well trained and well behaved, stood right where they had been reined in. Only the cottonwood trees, their branches blushing a pale early green, moved in the wind.

The silence was so unnatural that Enid wondered why Julian didn't simply pull the trigger and release them from this moment's bondage.

Mr. Garling said, "A pistolero too, I see."

"By God," Julian said, laughing softly, "you are a talker."

"Daughter," her father spoke very slowly, "you could tell him to put that pistol up."

Julian kept the pistol trained on Mr. Garling, but he turned his head slightly to look at Enid.

"I can't tell him what to do," she said to her father.

She wondered if Julian would ever shave his mustache; if he did then she could be certain, in moments like this, whether that was a smile playing at the corners of his lips.

Her father spoke again. "If you expect me to bless this union, sir, I will not do it. Not even at gunpoint."

Julian laughed louder this time. "Maybe it's your soul you ought to be thinking about blessing." He transferred the gun to his other hand and picked up the reins. "What I expect you to do is to let go of my team. Let go and stand aside. I don't give a good goddamn what else you do."

Mr. Garling jerked his hand away as if the harness leather was a hot wire.

Julian gestured with the gun. "The other."

Enid's father backed up until he stumbled on the edge where the road's hardpan began to erode into the soft dirt of the river bank.

"Can you drive a team?" Julian asked.

It took Enid a moment before she realized he was speaking to her. "I never have," she answered.

"Just grab hold of the reins. Not tight. Give them some slack. Bounce the reins up and down a couple times. They know what to do." Then—was he speaking to Enid's father?—he said, "I never whipped a horse in my life."

Enid did as he told her. She was startled when the horses responded immediately and stepped forward in unison. Enid wanted to look back at her father one more time—was that a new suit he was wearing?—but the horse's hooves were already striking the boards of the bridge, and she thought she needed to watch the road.

Julian called out to her father, "You let us know when you want to pay us a visit. Our home is always open to family!" The wheels rumbled across the bridge, and Julian shouted once more, "You know where to find me!"

Enid doubted she would ever see her father again.

Just after sundown the wind shifted and began to gust out of the northwest. The temperature fell, and a light rain slanted down. The rain soon turned to snow, and Enid had to wrap up in a blanket to shield herself from the sting of the icy pellets. When they finally rolled into Williston, Julian said to her, "Well, we made it, Wife. The prairie didn't get us this time." Enid was so cold the hinges of her jaw felt frozen, and she couldn't even get out the two words she had in mind to say: *This time?*

They checked into the Lewis and Clark Hotel, and after thawing out in front of one of the two big parlor stoves in the lobby, they went into the dining room, almost deserted on that Saturday night.

Enid was ravenous, and she ate a steak as large as Julian's. For dessert the waiter brought Julian a large slice of chocolate cake, which he ate but found unsatisfactory. "Should have brought one of them pies from the wedding," he said. "Can't beat the cooking of the Roosian girls." Neither of them said a word about meeting her father at the bridge.

With the meal Enid had her first taste of whiskey. She was reluctant to take a drink, but Julian insisted. She knew he wanted her to drink so he could do what he had in mind to do once they went upstairs. She was embarrassed to drink in public, but Julian assured her that anyone who saw her would know she was just trying to take the chill off the night.

Enid had seen men toss whiskey back and then shudder as if they had stepped into icy water, but she swallowed the liquor with ease. Of course, Julian mixed hers with coffee and sugar, but still, the whiskey seemed to do nothing but warm her chest. After her first cup she asked for another, and by the time they went upstairs she felt as though she had finally found a way to take a step back from her own life.

Their room was on the north side of the hotel, and the wind made the window vibrate and hum in its casement. Julian pulled the shade and drew the curtains. He turned to Enid and said, "You can prepare yourself right here. I'm going down the hall for a moment." His voice sounded deeper, thicker, than it normally did, but Enid attributed this—as she was ready to do for every departure from the usual—to whiskey. When he left the room he locked the door behind him.

Enid undressed slowly, and as she did, she folded each item—her blouse and skirt, her petticoat, her corset, her chemise—and put it in the armoire. It was important to her that Julian not see any of her undergarments. She had brought a union suit, and tomorrow if it was still cold, as she expected it would be, she would wear that. She congratulated herself for having packed it. Then she put on the nightgown that she and her mother had bought. Her flesh still felt sensitive from the cold, and the nightgown's crocheted yoke chafed her chest and back.

Enid lay down on the bed and adjusted the pillows behind her head. She looked down toward the foot of the bed, and it seemed unusually far away. Was this bed longer than most, or was this an illusion, the effect of lying alone in a bed large enough for two?

She could face what was to come. How bad could it be? If what happened between a man and a woman in the marriage bed was so unpleasant, there wouldn't be as many children in the world as there were. Besides, this was the day when she had looked at her father while he was in the sights of another man's gun. She had been ready for what would follow. She hadn't screamed or wept or pleaded for her father's life or tried to wrest the pistol from the man's—why couldn't she say it?—from her *husband's* hand. Instead, she had sat quietly on the buggy seat and thought the coldest thought of her life: if you are aiming at the V where my father's tie enters his vest, you are aiming too high. If she could bear up under the weight of that moment, she could certainly bear the weight of a man's body on hers.

Enid closed her eyes. The darkness swam with motion,

tilting and turning in one direction and then another, but she believed this sensation, too, was caused by the whiskey. She moved her head off the pillow so she could listen for her husband's approach with both ears. Then she realized: she was listening for the thud of his boots, and he would not be wearing them.

Thanksgiving
(1927)

❀ ❀ ❀

WESLEY Hayden unfolded the letter from his mother in order to read it one more time. The train was crossing a trestle and swayed from side to side even more than usual. He steadied the page on his leg. He had received the letter a week earlier; it was dated November 17, 1927:

"Dear Wesley, I'm so pleased that both my boys will be home for Thanksgiving. As you grow older and stray further from the nest, I worry about the day when neither you nor your brother will return for the holidays. I know the day will come when you and Frank will have your own homes and families but until then pardon me for selfishly wanting you here as often as possible."

Wesley was returning to his home in Bentrock, Montana, from Grand Forks, North Dakota, where he was a freshman at the University of North Dakota. His brother Frank, who was already home, was a junior at the University of Minnesota. The brothers had planned on traveling together—meeting in Fargo, North Dakota, and riding the train together to Bentrock—but Frank had found an early ride that would take him all the way to Miles City, so Wesley was left to ride the train alone.

The train lurched, the sound of the wheels on the track

changed, dropping an octave, and their speed altered slightly, like a horse changing its gait from a trot to a canter. They were off the trestle, and Wesley returned to his mother's letter.

"I saw Iris the other day, and she asked about you and said how much she missed you. She wanted to know if you'd be coming home for Thanksgiving. She was so excited to hear that you would be that I went ahead and invited her to share our meal with us. I hope that's all right. I know you're a college man now, but I didn't think you'd mind seeing Iris again. She looked so pretty in her red wool coat. . . ."

Wesley stopped reading and put the letter back in its envelope and stuck it inside his coat pocket. He had read far enough.

It was true, he had not written to Iris, and he had especially not told her he would be returning for Thanksgiving. He had hoped he would be able to avoid seeing her while he was home.

Wesley Hayden and Iris Heil had been a steady couple during Wesley's senior year in high school. She was the first girl Wesley kissed, the first girl to allow him to touch her bare breasts, and the first girl Wesley loved.

Nevertheless, when Wesley left for college he believed he was saying farewell to Iris for good. He did not relish the idea; when he said good-bye it was all he could do to hold back the tears, and the lump in his throat grew so large it seemed to tighten his chest until he could barely draw a breath.

But Wesley had ideas about leaving Bentrock, Montana, the town in which he was born and raised, for good. Going away to college was only the first step. Unlike his brother Frank, who was offered an athletic scholarship to play baseball at the University of Minnesota, Wesley had no financial incentive to choose a college outside his home state; he could as easily have boarded a train to go to Montana State in Bozeman or the university in Missoula, but he figured that if he was serious about making his life elsewhere he had to begin sometime.

Love was not the issue. Wesley loved Montana. He loved his parents. He supposed he even loved Iris. In the last few months, away from his home state for the longest stretch in his eighteen years, he had come to realize how much of it he treasured—its endless horizon, its huge sky, the way the air smelled faintly of sage and washed rock.

But Wesley's father, Julian Hayden, was an important man in their part of northeastern Montana. He was a landowner of modest wealth; he had substantially expanded his land holdings from his original homestead and supplemented them with a few buildings and businesses in town.

Of more significance, however, was the fact that Wesley's father was the county sheriff, and his hands controlled the gears of the county's political machinery. In short, the Hayden name was known, it meant something to virtually all the region's residents, and even if Wesley himself was not always sure of what it meant to be a Hayden, that didn't lessen the fact that as long as he lived in Bentrock he would automatically have an identity that he had nothing to do with forming.

And once he was out of his hometown and living in Grand Forks, Wesley felt a strange thrill in his anonymity. It was something he hadn't expected and certainly had never experi-

137

enced. He could walk around campus, and he was nobody—
just one more student in the throng that moved from building
to building. Or he could leave the college grounds and walk
down University Avenue until he came to the business district.
There he would not even be recognized as a student—he could
be a clerk in a shoe store, a vagrant, a soda jerk at Kemmel-
man's Pharmacy.

As he walked around the city, Wesley was careful to vary
his route, never to frequent the same store on consecutive
days, for fear he would become known as a regular. Many of
the other freshman males were being rushed by fraternities,
but Wesley had no interest in pledging. Then he'd be a Sigma
Chi or a Phi Delt. That was not for him. He had friends on
campus, his roommate and a few other fellows from his dor-
mitory, but he told them almost nothing of his background. A
classmate found out where Wesley was from and began to call
him "Montana." One night as a group of students walked back
from the library together, Wesley separated this young man
from the others and asked him if he wouldn't please use his
proper name. There must have been some pleading quality in
Wesley's voice or a beseeching look in his eyes, because the
student apologized and said he'd stop.

But now the train's engine was steaming relentlessly west-
ward, and sometime around midnight the train would pull
into Bentrock's depot. Wesley would step onto the platform
and then he'd be home again, a Hayden, and if his father or
brother were not yet there to pick him up, he would carry his
satchel into the brightly lit station. There he would doubtless
see Ray Hoffman, the Northern Pacific ticket agent. Ray

would greet him, welcome him home for Thanksgiving and ask, because he knew exactly how long Wesley had been gone and where he had been, how college was going in North Dakota. . . .

The meal was finished, but no one made a move to rise from the table. Wesley's father had carved the turkey, and its carcass still sat near his place. Occasionally Mr. Hayden reached out and pinched another small scrap of meat from the bones.

From her end of the table Wesley's mother said softly to her husband, "If you're still hungry, I have more turkey in the icebox. I put some away for the boys' sandwiches, but you're welcome to it."

Mr. Hayden shoved the turkey platter. "No, go on. Get it out of here."

Mrs. Hayden rose and began to stack plates and dishes.

Iris stood as well.

"You sit right back down," Wesley's mother said.

"I can help," Iris said.

"Absolutely not. You're a guest at our table, and we do not put our guests to work. You sit here and pretend you're hanging on every word these men speak."

Obediently Iris sat back down, and as she did she smiled sweetly at Wesley. He had his elbows on the table and his hands clasped in front of him. Iris reached out a finger and ran it slowly across the knuckles of his left hand, a gesture that felt so shockingly intimate that Wesley took his hand away. He picked up his water glass and turned his attention back to his father, who was telling a story about a man he had recently arrested.

But Wesley had difficulty concentrating on anything other than Iris. The only illumination in the dining room came from the candles on the table, and their wavering and flickering light softened and shadowed every smooth surface—the porcelain milk pitcher, the china bowls and platters, the faces of these people. Iris looked even lovelier than Wesley remembered. Something had changed in her since he had left, barely three months ago. She had lost something—a plumpness in her cheeks, a fullness around her mouth—and this absence made her look older. Her beauty now seemed permanent, no longer something that belonged only to her youth. Her dress was dark red with a white lace collar. Wesley remembered her wearing the dress to the school's Christmas dance the previous year. Tonight, however, in the room's dim light, the dress looked the color of wine. She was also wearing the necklace that Wesley had given her last Christmas, a thin gold chain holding a rhinestone framed by tiny pearls in the shape of a heart. Iris often fingered the pendant and then, as if she suddenly remembered she wasn't supposed to touch it, let it fall back against her throat and folded her hands on her lap. But it wasn't long before she was touching it again, running the rhinestone heart back and forth on its chain.

Wesley's father spoke louder, as if commanding his son's attention were merely a matter of his voice's volume. Perhaps it was. Wesley began to listen to his father's story.

"I was ready to haul him in," his father said. "Bring him up on a federal offense and everything, when he told me he was going to quit opening envelopes as soon as he came up with enough money for the meal. And if he read any letter that had important news, he'd see to it they got their mail. He'd deliver it himself.

"But I kept on driving. And then I hear sniffling and I look over and Emil's got tears running down his cheeks. Making a clean little track through the dirt.

"That did it. I pull over to the side of the road and say to him, Goddamn it, Emil, this is no way to be putting food on the table. Not at Thanksgiving, not at any time. Hell, it's not even a sensible way to steal. This part of the country, you could open a thousand envelopes and never come across so much as a dollar. But then Emil's another one of those Roosians who's none too bright. He couldn't quite put it all together to stick up a filling station. No, hell no. He's got to snatch the mail bag.

"So I let the sorry bastard go. Told him he was going to have to help Lonnie deliver the mail. If Lonnie would have him. Then I kicked his sorry ass out of the car and shooed him on home. He's goddamn lucky to be spending the night in his own bed."

Wesley's father turned to Iris and wagged his finger at her. "When you're around me, young lady," he said, "you're going to have to cover your ears. I'm too old to start watching my tongue."

Wesley's father got up and went to the sideboard. He opened the cupboard down below and brought out a bottle of sour mash bourbon, a gift brought all the way from Louisiana by Merle Dennis, an oil speculator who used Bentrock as a base while he ranged from southern Montana up through western North Dakota and into Canada searching for likely locations to drill for oil. Sheriff Hayden had served as Merle Dennis's unofficial guide through the territory, introducing him to ranchers and farmers and even helping him negotiate a few sales of mineral rights. In return for these favors, every time Merle Dennis came back to Bentrock he brought a gift for the sheriff—a hand-tooled belt, a jackknife with an ivory scrimshaw handle, a humidor of cigars, a card of hand-tied flies, a bottle of bourbon. Mr. Hayden put the bottle on the dining room table, and the candlelight gave the whiskey an amber glow. Mr. Hayden also put three cut-glass whiskey tumblers on the table.

"Now then," he said to his sons, "who would like to follow that delicious dinner with a swallow of fine whiskey?"

Wesley and Frank exchanged glances. They knew their father was referring to them. Iris was excluded from his offer by her age and gender. Wesley was sure their father knew his sons drank, but they had never been allowed to drink openly, much less at the family table. What had changed since Wesley left? Did attending college suddenly mean they were at an age to share their father's whiskey?

Frank did not hesitate. He picked up a glass and held it out for his father to fill. "And I bet you gave Emil a couple bucks, didn't you?" he said to his father.

Mrs. Hayden reentered the room. "It was more than a couple."

Mr. Hayden waved his hand dismissively. "I gave him ten. Told him to get his family a decent meal for Thanksgiving. And if I heard he bought a bottle with it, I'd throw his ass in jail."

While his father was pouring, Wesley offered his glass. His father poured in about two fingers of bourbon.

"Tell me," Frank asked his father, "who's sheriff now— you or Len? I've lost track."

Mercer County had a limit on the number of terms a sheriff could serve consecutively, and to get around this regulation, Len McAuley, Julian Hayden's deputy, served an occasional term as sheriff and designated Mr. Hayden as his deputy. Those were their official titles, but their actual duties did not change. No one had any doubts about who was in charge in Mercer County.

"Still me," Mr. Hayden said. "Election's next year. I've got another year in office."

Wesley brought the whiskey to his lips. As he did, its aroma, redolent of caramel and burnt wood, rushed up his nostrils. He hesitated before he drank, and then did so cautiously, hoping to avoid the effects the first swallow of whiskey could bring—an involuntary shudder, watering eyes, and, worst of all, a gasp or cough. The last thing Wesley wanted was for his father or brother or Iris to think he couldn't take a drink of whiskey without it stealing his breath away. He needn't have worried; the whiskey had the expected kick but it seemed cushioned—whiskey wrapped in soft cotton.

Mrs. Hayden stacked another armload of dirty dishes.

Wesley noticed her raise her eyebrows when she saw the tumblers of whiskey, but she said nothing.

"Where are your manners, son?" Mr. Hayden asked Wesley. "Aren't you going to offer this young lady a taste?" He raised his own glass to indicate that Iris might like some bourbon.

Iris wrinkled her nose. "I wouldn't want any."

But now Wesley had to make the offer; his father was giving him a lesson that he had to learn.

He held his glass out to Iris. "Would you like to try a sip?"

Frank lightly slapped his brother on the arm. "Maybe she wants her own glass."

"Would you?"

Iris shook her head. "I don't even like the smell."

"This is different," Mr. Hayden said. "This is as good as whiskey gets."

Iris continued to shake her head. "My dad let me take a sip of his whiskey once. It burned my throat."

Frank said, "Your old man never had twelve-year-old bourbon like this in the house." Frank looked over at his father so abruptly Wesley wondered if his father had kicked Frank under the table.

"You can't swallow liquor like water," Mr. Hayden scolded. "Especially not fine whiskey like this. If you just throw it back you're not doing it justice." He raised his glass and sipped slowly. When he took the glass away he kept his lips pursed; the whiskey was obviously still in his mouth. Then he inhaled deeply, as if swallowing whiskey was done with the nose. He licked his lips and sighed. "By God, whoever made this knows a hell of a secret."

Mr. Hayden looked to his sons before offering his next advice. "Now, if you're drinking the bootleg liquor you get around here, you might as well hold your nose and get it down as quick as you can. Then hope you don't go blind. Or worse."

His father reached past Wesley and held out his own glass to Iris. "Go ahead and try some, Miss. Like I told you. Just take a small sip and roll it around in your mouth a little before you swallow."

Iris looked at Wesley but before he could speak or register any expression, she took the tumbler from his father.

"Sure, go ahead," Frank said. "We're not going to tell your folks."

For Wesley's family, like most others in their part of Montana, Prohibition was something to be got around rather than observed. There were plenty of nondrinkers, but their abstinence was more likely for religious rather than legal reasons. Certainly, Sheriff Hayden made no special effort to enforce the 18th amendment unless some bootlegger tried to take undue advantage of the county's citizens. Wesley couldn't remember seeing his own mother take a drink of whiskey. She would have an occasional glass of sweet wine, and on hot summer evenings she might share her husband's beer, but hard liquor—Wesley didn't think so. He was quite sure he had never seen his father offer his mother a drink of whiskey.

Iris lifted the glass to her lips. Before she drank she said to Frank, "You *better* not tell."

Her eyelids fluttered and almost closed. According to Mr.

Hayden's instructions, she held the liquor in her mouth for a moment, but when she swallowed it was with such noticeable effort that it seemed to take muscular strength to get the whiskey down.

Iris shuddered as if a draft from an open window had reached her. She twisted her mouth down. "Ugh!" Wesley's father and brother laughed at her reaction.

Why the act, Wesley wondered. He had seen Iris drink— wine, beer, and hard liquor—at parties. Just last summer, on a sweltering day, Wesley remembered, he and Iris had gone swimming in the Knife River, and Wesley had brought along two quarts of homemade beer. While they swam, the beer chilled in the river water. When they got out of the water, they opened both bottles, one for each of them, and Iris finished her bottle well before Wesley finished his. The ice-cold beer gave him a headache, so he gave Iris what was left in his bottle. She drank that down as quickly as she had her own. Admittedly, Wesley was not just being generous in offering her more beer.

They had been going further and further with their sexual experiments, and Wesley had a notion that perhaps that day he and Iris would actually have intercourse. The conditions seemed perfect: they were both in bathing suits, Iris was in an especially playful and affectionate mood, and perhaps with enough beer in her. . . .

For shade and privacy they crawled up under the bridge where it was dark and cool, even on the summer's hottest day. Years of the river rising and falling, rushing and slowing, had weathered the beams and timbers of the bridge until they felt soft to the touch. Even the boulders and concrete pilings were furred with moss. The Indians who fished the Knife River's deep holes or the fast water in the spring had cleared away the brush and arranged logs under the bridge, so it was easy to find a place to sit. Or lie down.

Wesley pushed his kisses harder and harder into Iris until she fell back under their pressure. She was still wet from their swim, and his hands slid across her skin as if she had been lubricated for his touch. Her wet hair smelled of river water and permanent wave solution.

He tried to get his hand inside the top of her bathing suit, but the angle was awkward and the wet fabric clung to her. Iris twisted away from his fumbling hands. Done for, Wesley thought. But then Iris astonished him.

She sat up straight and, with what seemed nothing more than a simple shrug of her shoulders, slipped her bathing suit down to uncover her breasts. She wriggled around until she got the suit down around her waist. Then she lay back, her torso exposed now to his sight as well as his touch.

For a moment, Wesley couldn't move. He had seen a woman's breasts before, but only in Tommy Salter's French postcards. Iris's breasts were small, and the nipples weren't much larger than pennies. Their dark skin was puckered and erect. He had felt those breasts only by reaching under layers of clothing and only in darkened rooms. For the moment he didn't want to do anything more than look at her—it was enough, it was too much—but he dimly knew that just staring was a violation of some etiquette that ruled moments like these.

He reached out for her, and as he did someone stepped onto the bridge above them. Whoever was crossing walked slowly and stayed close to the rail. When the walker came to the center of the bridge he stopped, gazing at the river below. He began to whistle a tune Wesley almost recognized. Wesley looked at Iris. She had made no move to cover herself, not with her bathing suit or her arms. In fact, she was trying not to laugh out loud.

The walker began again, and soon his steps no longer echoed on the bridge planks.

Immediately Iris stood, balanced on a rock, and jumped up to grab one of the bridge's iron cross braces. She pulled herself up until she could see above the bridge. "Who the hell was that?" she asked.

Wesley just sat there, staring at her once again, but this time with another brand of amazement. Who was this girl, hanging there, her breasts exposed to the summer air? He suddenly felt as though he didn't know her at all—could never know her. How could he have dared to put his hands all over her?

She was Iris Heil, the only girl in a family of five children. Was that how she had gained the strength to chin herself like that, from trying to keep up with her older brothers? Another disquieting thought occurred to him. Surely her brothers had seen her breasts, and perhaps so frequently she had no hesitation or shame in revealing herself to Wesley.

Still holding onto the brace, Iris lowered herself, the hard, bunched muscles in her arms and shoulders stretching and thinning. She must have seen something in Wesley's eyes

148

because she did not come back to him under the bridge. She pulled her bathing suit back up and adjusted its straps on her shoulders. "Are we going back in the water?" she asked.

Without waiting for his answer, she picked her way among the rocks until she was above a pool deep enough for swimmers to dive into. She leaped awkwardly, all arms and legs, and as she vanished underwater, Wesley felt as though he had a new knowledge of loss: when opportunities that will never come again slip away untouched.

In the months that followed, Wesley was haunted by the memory of that day down by the river. But the image that kept recurring wasn't of Iris in his arms but of her swinging from the bridge's cross brace like a beautiful, half-naked trapeze artist. Even in his mind she was there for him to see but not to touch.

Now, Iris put the whiskey glass back on the table and lifted her fingers to her lips as if to wipe away the bourbon's heat. "I don't see how you can drink *that*," she said.

Wesley looked away, disgusted with Iris's hypocrisy. He glanced into the kitchen, where his mother was cleaning up after the meal. At that moment she was not working. She held a dish towel in her hands, bunched like a bouquet of coarse cloth. Wesley's mother was staring into the room where her husband was teaching an underage woman how to drink sour mash whiskey. When Wesley's eyes and his mother's met, she turned away and went back to her work.

"It'll put hair on your chest," Wesley's brother teased Iris. "Look out!"

"That old wives' tale," she said and turned back to Wesley.

What was the look in her eyes? Was she asking him for help? Did she want him to take her away? Or was she enjoying the attention and did she only want him not to give her away as she pretended, for his father and brother, to be someone she was not?

"Then you better pour yourself another glass," Wesley said to his brother. "You need all the help you can get."

"Hey, brother. You don't want to get into a hair-counting contest. You'll lose for sure." Frank laughed the same easy laugh that Wesley had spent hours alone trying to emulate.

Wesley pointed to Frank's glass. "You going to drink that?"

"You want to make a contest out of that, too?"

"I'm just asking."

Mr. Hayden leaned toward Iris. "Your brothers get along like this?"

Iris wrinkled her nose the way she did after drinking the whiskey. "All the time."

Frank waved his hand as if his brother was not worth his time or energy. Then he directed his attention back to Iris. "Pretty necklace you have there," Frank said.

Iris smiled at Wesley. "Wesley gave it to me."

"Is that right?" Frank moved his chair closer to Iris. "Where'd you get the good taste to pick out something that nice, little brother?"

"Maybe you got some help from your mother, eh?" Mr. Hayden suggested.

Wesley was about to deny that he had had his mother's aid when Iris volunteered, "I might have given him a hint or two."

A hint or two. Last year in the month before Christmas, Wesley and Iris walked downtown every day after school, ostensibly to meet their friends at Douglas's Rexall for Cokes or phosphates. But the real reason for the daily excursions, Wesley came to know, was to provide Iris with more opportunities to stop in front of the window of Hesvig's Jewelry and point out the necklace she loved and wanted so badly she was "ready to throw a rock through the window and just grab it for herself." When he gave her the necklace for Christmas, Iris couldn't even pretend to be surprised.

"Can I get a closer look?" Frank asked Iris.

She looked down and pushed her chest out slightly but made no move to lift the necklace for Frank's inspection.

She didn't have to. Frank picked it up for himself. He did not pick it up with his thumb and index finger, as he would if he were lifting a pebble from the floor. He slid four fingers under the pendant and held the necklace in his palm.

What bothered Wesley most was the fact that Frank didn't lift the necklace from Iris's chest. He simply held it there, the gold chain and rhinestones glittering in the candlelight, and the back of his hand resting on the swell of Iris's bosom.

The thought suddenly occurred to Wesley—had Frank had his hand there before? Had Frank touched Iris's breasts before Wesley ever did? Was that why both Iris and Frank could

151

act so calmly now—Frank because there was nothing new about having his hand there and Iris because she had allowed Frank to touch her before? Perhaps that day down at the river Iris thought nothing of letting Wesley see her breasts because she had already revealed them to his brother?

Still holding the necklace, Frank said to his father, "Here, take a look. See what your son is spending his money on." Frank looked up at Wesley. "Or is it Dad's money?"

Mr. Hayden rose from his chair and leaned forward. Now he too had his face directed toward Iris's breasts. He tilted his head to one side, then the other, no doubt appraising the pendant and its setting, but he could as easily have been eyeing the young woman's breasts.

"Lovely," Mr. Hayden said.

Wesley felt ready to explode. In his rage he was ready to smash his fists into his father's and brother's faces, to knock them to the floor and kick them until they lost consciousness and couldn't even flinch from his blows, until kicking them would be like kicking a sack of grain. Then Wesley would step down on his brother's hand, the hand that tenderly held Iris's necklace, and with his boot heel he would grind away until Frank's finger bones gave way, cracking against the floorboards.

Of course Wesley did nothing. The candlelight stirred from an unseen movement of air, and the shadows in the corners shifted shape. His father had leaned his palm on the table, and Wesley noticed the cross-hatching of black hair on his father's muscular forearm. He heard Iris's breathing, short and quick—was she unnerved because she was pinned down by these two men or did their attention excite her?

Wesley looked around for help—would his mother be coming back into the room soon? No, she didn't know what was happening in her house. At some time in the last few minutes she had closed the swinging door separating the kitchen and the dining room. Did she close it, Wesley wondered, because she somehow knew what was happening and chose not to be a witness and therefore not responsible?

In desperation, Wesley stood and wedged his way between Iris and his father and brother.

Mr. Hayden and Frank both leaned away from Iris, although Frank took the necklace with him for an instant, only reluctantly letting it fall back on her chest.

Wesley grabbed the whiskey bottle as if that was what he was after all along. He poured himself a drink more generous than the one his father had given him.

"Generally you ask," his father said, "before you help yourself to another man's whiskey."

Before he answered his father, Wesley took a drink of bourbon. But in his anger and haste he swallowed too much, and he had to struggle to keep from coughing. He squinted his eyes to prevent the sudden tears from spilling over.

"I guess I figured," Wesley said as gravely as he could, "we shared everything in this house."

Wesley's father pushed himself back from the table as if he needed to get a better look at this son of his who stood over him drinking his whiskey.

"You either forgot some of your manners at that university," Mr. Hayden said, "or I fouled up and let you go when

153

you still had something left to learn."

"Don't worry about it. You taught me. I learned by example."

Mr. Hayden leaned back even further, as though his son had still not come into focus. "I believe worrying about it is exactly what I should be doing, young man."

Wesley had the feeling that his father was only distracting him, that while they locked stares across the table, Frank and Iris were exchanging looks of a friendlier sort.

He broke eye contact with his father and turned his attention quickly back to Iris. "We have to go," he said, his voice harsher than he intended it to sound.

But Iris was staring up at him as though she was not quite certain of his identity either. He couldn't blame her; at that moment he wasn't sure himself.

There was a wet ring on the white tablecloth where earlier his glass of ice water had rested. Now Wesley set his whiskey down, aiming the heavy glass for that same damp circle. Once the glass was out of his hand, he watched the whiskey for a moment, trying to judge the steadiness of his hand by how much the amber liquid shimmered in the candlelight.

"Let's go," he said again. This time his voice was softer, and Iris rose immediately.

Mr. Hayden stood too. He pushed his chair in and stepped to the side. He thrust his chest out, and for a moment Wesley thought his father was blocking his way, trying to prevent his son from taking this young woman away. But Julian Hayden always rose when a woman, young or old, stood, and he liked to take up the slack in his suspenders by puffing out his chest.

Frank said, "Oh, come on, Wes. Jesus. Wait up."

But Wesley did not wait. He guided Iris gently toward the door. His only hesitation as they left the dining room was to glance back toward the kitchen and his mother. The door was still closed.

It was snowing as they left the house, heavy wet flakes that were so large in the night sky that Wesley didn't have to look to the porch light to see them fall. He gazed straight up, and there they came, a riot of white scraps falling so swiftly it seemed there must be more to them than mere water, ice, and air.

Iris walked ahead of him on her way to the car, and Wesley could tell by the length and pace of her stride that she was angry. Or perhaps it was not anger at all but puzzlement. How many times over the months they had been dating had she looked at him and said, "I just don't understand you." And the implication was always clear: the fault was in Wesley, not in her ability to understand.

The snow was already working hard to fill in Iris's tracks, and for a moment Wesley stopped and watched her walk on without him. Flakes of snow caught in her hair and on the dark wool of her coat. He turned and looked back toward the house and their dark footsteps trailing across the yard. If the snow continued to fall at this pace, in less than an hour you wouldn't be able to tell that anyone had ever left that house.

Len McAuley

(1935)

❀ ❀ ❀

L EN McAuley had his first drink of liquor when he was only twelve years old. The drink was given him by Dr. Wright, who hoped the liquor would help the boy make it through his second day in Montana. The doctor poured three fingers of bourbon, filled the glass with water, and then dropped in a sugar cube. "I've got no medicine for your kind of pain, son," the doctor said, "but this helps some folks."

Len drank the whiskey down in three swallows. He didn't know if it helped or not, but from that day on whiskey and water became his drink of choice. From time to time he even sweetened it with sugar—and brought back his childhood with the first sip. On most days, Len used whiskey exactly the way Dr. Wright originally prescribed it: to help him through the pain of each day in Montana.

Len McAuley came to Mercer County, Montana, in 1898 with his father, mother, and older brother. As soon as school was out for the summer, they left their home in St. Paul, Minnesota, planning to homestead in northeast Montana. By the time they got off the train, gathered their luggage and belongings, and arranged to rent a wagon to haul everything out to their section of land, the hour was late, and Mr. McAuley was afraid he might have trouble finding their claim in the dark. They decided to spend the night at the Carson House Hotel.

During the night, a fire began. The cause was never determined—a kerosene lamp knocked over, a traveling salesman's cigar left smoldering—but the hotel, built of lumber from forests in the Judith Mountains, burned so quickly that the local fire brigade was reduced to watching the fire burn itself out and making certain the flames did not spread to adjacent stores or buildings.

Len never knew for sure whether it was his father, mother, or older brother who threw him out their second-story hotel room window, breaking Len's arm but saving his life. In his memory of that night, it seemed to Len that he fell through the flames, and that as the building fell in on itself he had simply ridden the thick cloud of smoke away from the flames and into the night sky. Only two other rooms besides the McAuleys' were occupied, one by the salesman and one by an older man who taught music in the local schools and lived, during the school year, in the hotel. Both these hotel patrons, along with three members of the McAuley family, perished in the fire. Only Len McAuley and the desk clerk escaped.

The Presbyterian minister and his wife offered to take Len into their home, since he had no other family, but he declined. He and his family had come to Montana to make a living from the land, and that was what he was determined to do. The citizens of Bentrock took up a collection for him, and he used that money along with what little he earned by selling off the family possessions that survived the fire, and bought a wagon, a horse, and supplies. As soon as he was able, he drove out to the land that his father had planned to farm. There young Len McAuley made his own home, as best he could. He lived at first under his wagon, filling in three sides with brush, rocks, and what wood he could find. At night he crawled in as though he were entering a cave. That suited him. If he lived like an animal, perhaps he would feel no more than an animal felt—heat, cold, hunger, fatigue—and the human emotions, sorrow and grief and loneliness, would leave him.

Of course he was too young to file a claim for eventual ownership of the land, but no one said anything because everyone was certain the boy would vacate the section before long. If the wind and the heat, then the cold and the snow did not drive him off the prairie, the isolation would.

But he stayed. He hunted, he fished, and he foraged for other food and firewood. The women of the county made sure that when they or their husbands passed anywhere near Len McAuley's claim, they dropped off food, especially the baked goods that they knew a boy would love but could never manage for himself. In fact, on his rudimentary cookstove Len had managed to make a kind of scone similar to the ones his mother made. He even used fresh-picked blueberries, an improvement, he felt, on his mother's recipe. He would accept these offerings but none of the invitations for a home-cooked meal at one of the nearby farms or ranches or in town.

Eventually he built himself a shack, little more than a lean-to, but which offered greater protection from the elements than his wagon allowed. The very first time he stood inside this home—stood upright and heard the wind turn away when it came to those walls of his making—something in him changed, and he felt the loss of human companionship like a physical pain, as though part of his being had been torn away. He rode that day to the nearest human habitation, a homestead less than a mile upstream from where he had been living.

There he met Julian Hayden, another teenage boy, and his mother. The Haydens had come to Montana from Iowa and had been living on their claim longer than Len, yet they still had that uncertain, unsettled look in their eyes and on their property that said that the very next hardship—whether as large as a hailstorm or as small as a rattlesnake—might be the one to drive them off the prairie for good.

Len had come there for company, but once there he found he had nothing to say. Finally, after an awkward silence during which Julian and his mother simply stared up at Len sitting bareback on his horse, Len blurted out, "Do you need any help?"

He had meant only to offer the kind of assistance that one neighbor offers another, but Julian misunderstood. He looked at his mother, the two of them conferred for a moment, and then Julian said, "We'll hire you."

That afternoon Len McAuley helped Julian Hayden put up a section of fence. He worked for Julian Hayden first on the ranch, and then years later when Julian moved into town and ran for county sheriff, Len became part of that partnership as well. Julian hired Len McAuley as his deputy, and when Julian's three allotted terms in office expired, Len served a term (with Julian as his deputy) until Julian was eligible to run again.

When Julian Hayden decided to go back to ranching, he turned his sheriff's badge over to his son, and Len gave his loyalty to another Hayden generation, serving this time as Wesley's deputy. The son needed Len more than his father ever had, for although Wesley had been born and raised in Mercer County, he never seemed to understand the region or its people the way his father had. Len reasoned that this was because Julian had been there almost as long as the county— they grew up together—and the boy came along after both were established. To help Wesley along, Len counseled him, "Just do what your dad would do," but the advice wasn't much use. Although Len instinctively knew what Julian would do in almost any situation, Julian's son seldom did.

In Len's mind the incident with the Eldridge boy illustrated this difference between father and son.

Jimmy Eldridge was not a bright boy. He was big for his age to begin with, and then he flunked a grade or two, which only emphasized the difference between him and his classmates. Other boys would tease Jimmy just to see him spit and sputter in his rage. One day when Wesley had been in office for less than a year, Jimmy got into it on the playground with two other boys. Young Miss Hauser tried to break up the fight. Jimmy was on top of George Flynn, and Miss Hauser tried to pull Jimmy off. Jimmy didn't turn around to look; he just threw his arm back to get this new attacker away. Miss Hauser went flying, and she hit her head on a rock. A scalp cut doesn't have to be very bad to bleed a lot, and she did.

Another teacher tried to stop the bleeding, but it was no use. Miss Hauser had to have a couple stitches in the back of her head. When Wesley Hayden heard about this incident he went off as though someone had been murdered. Len tried to calm him down, but Wesley kept saying, over and over, "A teacher. We can't stand for this happening to one of our teachers."

Once Wesley got the details, or as many as he wanted to hear, he drove over to the Eldridge home. He took Jimmy out of the house, loaded him into the car—the car with the official insignia on the door, so everyone in the neighborhood knew who was taking Jimmy away—and drove him down to the jail. He didn't actually put the boy in a cell, but he brought him to the open door, let him have a good look at that dark interior, and told Jimmy that he could be locked up for what he did in the school yard. Then he let the boy sit in the office for an hour before he took him home.

Len knew Wesley was trying to handle the problem the way his father would have—by acting quickly and decisively, trying to teach the boy a lesson he wouldn't forget, but still keeping the affair out of court. But Wesley didn't get a damn thing right.

If he had known the Eldridge family, he would have known something about their pride. Jimmy was the youngest child in a family of five, and the only one who was not as bright and handsome as a newly minted silver dollar, and his parents would prefer as little attention come to him as possible. Wesley's father would have called Jimmy's father, told him about the playground incident, and then forgotten about it, sure that Mr. Eldridge would speak to his boy and that nothing like it would happen again. Julian could also be sure that the Eldridges would cast their votes for Julian (or for Len) in the next election.

But perhaps it was so much easier for Len to know what Julian Hayden would do because Len had devoted so many days and hours of his life studying Julian Hayden, letting that man's surety answer for the doubt and uncertainty in Len's own life. Len had attached himself and his fortunes to Julian Hayden, for better or for worse. He had let Julian serve as his polestar, giving him direction where he had none. When Julian decided to marry, to bring a wife to his ranch, Len looked around until he found a woman for himself—Daisy Pender, a sheep rancher's daughter from nearby Franklin County.

Daisy talked so much that Len didn't propose to her the night he planned to. He simply couldn't find enough space in all her talk, talk, talk to squeeze in his question. Two nights later he got the matter taken care of and then only by first directing her attention to the western horizon. "Look!" he shouted, as if something was out there that human eyes had never seen. When she looked in that direction he used the pause to ask her to marry him. She said yes. And more. On the heels of her assent, Daisy resumed her talking and out tumbled all her plans for their life together. Len couldn't be sure if she was making up these plans as she spoke, or if she had anticipated his question and worked all this out long in advance. For a while he listened to her, then he leaned back and concentrated on his hands.

When it was not possible for Len to take a drink to transport himself out of an uncomfortable moment—as most moments in human company were for him—he had developed a mannerism that sometimes worked almost as well as whiskey. He would loosely lace together three fingers from his left hand with three fingers from his right. He left his thumbs and index fingers free. Then he lightly touched the tips of those four fingers together, lining them up so each touched its mate in exactly the same place, so that each line and groove of skin had its precise match. This simple action gave him inordinate satisfaction, as if something were being restored, resolved, in the instant when the fingertips touched.

He returned his attention to Daisy just as she was saying that she was "not one of those women who avoids her wifely duties." She had been around men enough to know what they required of a wife, and she would not back off from any part of the contract. Len leaned further back into the porch's shade so Daisy would not see him blush.

Over the years, Len did not often ask Daisy to perform those duties. Shortly after they were married something happened to the way Len thought of her. She became like a relative to him, perhaps a cousin he had known since childhood. It even seemed sometimes as though she had been waiting for him in Montana, a member of the McAuley clan sent out ahead of the others to scout out the territory. Then he tried to wave away those notions as if they were haze, smoke, fumes escaping from an uncorked whiskey bottle. She was a Pender, daughter of Amos and Harriet, both from Montana sheepherding families.

At times Len considered that the problem was in him, that he was simply not capable of feeling for a woman what he was supposed to feel. Daisy said she knew what men required—well, Len knew too. For much of his life he had been hearing their conversations—in saloons, in barbershops, around the cattle pens. He had heard them talk about women as though they were prey to be stalked, surprised, and then brought to their knees or thrown onto their backs. For many men it seemed as though they couldn't take their pleasure unless it brought pain to a woman. Len wanted no part of the deed or the talk. It was another reason he preferred to do his drinking at home or in his office late at night.

Then a young woman came to town, and Len knew he could feel what other men felt.

She was from eastern North Dakota, a farm girl just a state away, yet it seemed as if she could have come from the other side of the earth. She was openhearted, soft-spoken, and well mannered. It was not that Montanans weren't capable of being gentle or kind, but this young woman acted as if those were qualities to be proud of rather than embarrassed about.

And yes, she was pretty, in a delicate, small-boned way. She also had an allure that reminded Len of a woman he had once seen when he was a boy.

His mother was a seamstress, and her customers often came to their apartment for fittings. One day Len's mother called him into the kitchen when she was working on a woman's dress. The woman was in the room, standing behind the screen his mother had set up in the corner. Len's mother wanted him to go to the store for thread because she was

167

about to run out, but Len could not tear his vision away from the screen where the woman was. All he could see was her arm, long and pale and bare and extended out from the screen as she waited for the garment that Len's mother was stitching. The woman's fingers were curved slightly, and from where Len stood it almost seemed as though she was gesturing to him. Even after his mother barked at him to carry out his errand, he could only back slowly from the room. Even after his mother was dead, and every spool of her thread gone up in flames with her, Len still carried with him the image of that naked arm.

Len McAuley did not see this gesture again until that young woman, new to Montana but already well on her way to befriending the entire community, signaled to him across the crowded coffee shop of the Northern Pacific Hotel. He had just climbed the stairs (the coffee shop looked down on the lobby from an open mezzanine), and he was trying not to be obvious about the fact that he was searching for her in the crowd. She saw him just as he saw her.

"Len! Len—over here!" And she stood and indicated with a graceful sweep that an empty place was available at her table. It was a morning in late June, the third consecutive day of the summer's first heat, and her slender arm was bare and pale. She worked all day in the Register of Deeds office, and the summer sun and wind did not have a chance to tan and dry her skin the way it did so many Montana women's.

If there was any portion of his heart she had not already seized, then that gesture completed the job. Sunlight poured through two high windows, and everything in the room—

cigarette smoke, dust motes, even the clatter of cups and saucers and ashtrays, the excited gabble that rose from the town's store and office workers as they gathered for their first break of the day—seemed to thicken, slow, and swirl in those shafts of light. Through the haze and din she had picked Len out and motioned him to her side. The feeling that suffused him told him what he had to do.

He walked to the bar where the coffee and tea pots and heavy china cups and saucers were lined up on white linen towels. He poured himself a cup of coffee, dropped a nickel in a wooden bowl (all the morning customers at the hotel were on the honor system), then turned and left the dining room without even tipping his hat to the woman who signaled to him. The woman he loved.

She was Gail Hayden, wife to Wesley and daughter-in-law to Julian. She worked in the Mercer County courthouse, and the sheriff's office was in the basement of the same building. Len saw her there. He saw her in the Northern Pacific Hotel dining room. He saw her playing shuffleboard with her husband in Vic's Bar on Main Street. He saw her out at the ranch at Hayden family gatherings. Finally, as if to emphasize the futility of trying to avoid this woman with whom he had foolishly allowed himself to fall in love, Len saw her in his own kitchen, his own living room. Wesley and his bride moved into a house right next to Len and Daisy's, and Daisy and Gail became good friends. Daisy introduced Gail around town, showed her where to buy her bread (Cox's Bakery, if she was not going to bake her own) and meat (Frechette's Butcher Shop), where to have her hair done, and where her husband was likely to be when he was neither at work nor at home (the High Line Billiard Parlor or McRae's Mobil Station).

Whenever Len walked into his house and saw Gail Hayden drinking coffee at the kitchen table, he was filled instantly with equal measures of joy and sadness. He was pleased to see her, even if it was only for the few minutes it took him to fill his cup, exchange a word or two about the weather, and retire to the living room, where, from his chair, he could hear every word of the conversation. But perhaps it was better if he did not see her so often, for he had no hope of purging himself of his feeling for her if it was constantly renewed by her smile, her voice. Her wave.

After Gail Hayden came to town, Len McAuley's consumption of alcohol during the day dropped almost to nothing. He didn't want to take a chance that she would see him drunk.

Late at night, however, after he finished his patrol, when Daisy was asleep, Len sat in the living room and drank whiskey until he could close his eyes and not see Gail Hayden's shy smile or her blue eyes or her small, straight teeth or her ankles that looked so thin Len was surprised they could support any weight at all. Those ankles that she often reached down to massage, but Len knew she was actually tugging her stockings, trying to pull the seams straight. When Len saw her do this, something in him caught and pulled tight, as if a cord ran from his throat to his groin. When she walked away, it was with just a little bobble in her gait, and Len wondered if it was those ankles again, or her high-heeled shoes.

Then, just when Len thought the whiskey oblivion was total, when he thought he could close his eyes to nothing but red shadows and smoke, there her arm would be, beckoning to him from the billowing darkness.

But Len hadn't been drinking whiskey all those years without learning something about its uses and its power. He had one more drink, as quick and raw as he could take it. Then he put two fingers to his closed eyes and pressed hard, harder. In another moment both thought and inner sight served this new pain. If his swirling head and stomach seemed up to making the trip, he would head for the bedroom. Many nights he didn't try and fell asleep in his chair.

Yet no matter how much whiskey he drank, no matter where he slept, he was always awake in time to watch Gail Hayden walk across the street from her house to the courthouse.

Len McAuley was not the only man who found Wesley Hayden's wife attractive. In the late spring an oilman came to Bentrock, up from Missouri or Mississippi, Len couldn't remember which. One of those southern states where people talked too much, and then made it worse by drawling out their words as if their mouths were for nothing but making noise.

This oil speculator, Gilbert Bennett, was a cocky little man who wore two-tone shoes and suits the color of Montana rock—pale gray granite or sandstone. He was supposed to be in the area to buy mineral rights, but as far as Len could see, the man didn't do much more than shake dice at the Silver Dollar Bar and flirt with the secretaries and the waitresses at the hotel dining room.

And of those women he singled out Gail Hayden to receive most of his attention. "Sunshine," he called her, saying that her smile was the only ray of sunshine in that Godforsaken part of the country. Gail blushed at the remark, and Len wondered if he should tell her he heard Bennett say the same damn thing to Mary Morrissey.

At first, Bennett was content to compliment Gail, and even then his flattery was directed at her character more than her appearance. Gradually, he became more personal. "Can you cook too? My God, what more could a man ask for—not only is she a beauty but she brings home a paycheck and puts food on the table." When Bennett saw Gail eating a piece of apple cake one morning, he rushed over to her table and pretended to pull the cake away from her. "Let's have none of this now. I don't want you eating anything that's going to ruin that pretty little figure." When he caught her staring out the window, he said, "I know, I know—there's not much to interest someone like you up in this corner of the world, is there? What say you leave that husband of yours and you and me will go off and find some excitement. God! there's no sadder sight than a beautiful woman bored."

After Bennett made a remark like this, he laughed his high-pitched little laugh. Gail Hayden blushed and managed a tight smile, but Len thought there was more discomfort than mirth in her eyes.

172

Len finally decided he should speak to the sheriff about Bennett.

"What do you think of that southerner?" Len asked Wesley one afternoon in the office while they were catching up on paperwork. Len had long known that the best way to give Wesley advice about his work was by circling around and coming in the back door. "He sure don't fit in around here, if you ask me."

"He's a character all right."

"I noticed he's mighty familiar around the women."

"For a little fellow he's got a lot of strut in him. I don't know where he gets it."

"Wherever. He's got his share and then some."

Wesley turned to his typewriter, rolled in a sheet of paper, and began to type, his index fingers tapping out words in sudden little bursts of speed. Len waited until Wesley paused. "Gail too."

Wesley kept his fingers on the keys. "What about Gail?"

"Like I say. The way he gets familiar."

"Is he bothering her, would you say?"

"Embarrassing her, more like."

Wesley nodded. "It's no secret when that happens. I don't know anybody gets as red." He resumed typing.

Len stood and walked around the office, staying close to the walls like a dog that has been scolded but still wants its master's attention. He stopped directly behind Wesley. "Maybe I should say something to him."

"About what?"

"His behavior around the ladies."

Wesley backed up the paper in the typewriter and leaned toward the sheet as if the answer to Len's question was printed there. "They're grown-up Montana women. They can take care of themselves. Gail too. Besides, what are you going to say to him? He hasn't broken any law."

Len stared at Wesley for a moment as he concentrated on aligning the paper in the machine. Neither Len nor Wesley smoked, but the basement office still smelled of the cigars Wesley's father smoked. Wesley's father—Len couldn't imagine that Julian Hayden would be hunched over a typewriter while Bennett—or *anyone*—was flirting with Bentrock's married women, much less his own daugher-in-law. He'd take that fellow aside and explain how things worked around here, how he'd best watch what he said to women who weren't free for his picking. If you're looking for that, you don't look in the direction of women who were already spoken for. Try that with some of the squaws from the reservation. Or some of the Russian farm girls. Or drive across the border to North Dakota and see if they like that kind of talk over there. Wesley's father wouldn't threaten Bennett. He wouldn't say, you stop this or else. He'd just explain. And Bennett would understand.

But Wesley wasn't his father.

As Len walked out of the office he heard the *zzzst* of a sheet of paper being pulled violently from the typewriter. He wasn't much of a typist either.

Then Len heard something, and he decided, no matter what Wesley said, no matter what the law read, Bennett had to be dealt with.

It happened on a Tuesday afternoon, again in the hotel coffee shop. Gail Hayden was there, sitting at a table with two other women who worked in the courthouse. The women finished their lunches, rose from the table, and began to walk toward the stairs. Gail stayed a moment longer at the table, drinking the last of her coffee and counting out a few coins for the waitress.

When she walked out, with that wobbling gait of hers, she went past Bennett and three other men who stood at the bar looking at a topographical map of their corner of Montana. The map was weighted down at each corner with a coffee cup. Bennett was explaining what the rises, dips, hills, and folds in the region might mean in terms of possible oil deposits. Then Gail passed, and Bennett stopped talking and watched her. He even leaned back from the bar so he could keep his eyes attached to her until she was completely out of sight. Then he turned to the other men and said, "But I can tell you where I'd like to drill."

Len was also standing at the bar, close enough to see and hear everything. After Bennett made this remark, Len paid very close attention to how the three men reacted. They all laughed, and Len silently recited their names to himself—Lyle Branch, Ray Hollister, Carl McCarty—committing them to memory and vowing that these men would meet with trouble at some future date.

Punishment in some indefinite future, however, would

175

not do for Bennett. That man needed to be stopped, before he said one more word, made one more gesture that would degrade a Bentrock woman.

Len considered walking over to Bennett right at that moment, accusing him of being the kind of trash that was not wanted in the community, and knocking him to the floor.

But that wouldn't do much more than make Len look like a bully, an unreasonable man abusing a stranger—and a man who could bring some economic good to their region at that. More likely, people would say—Len, drunk at noon and striking that oilman. And he's a law enforcement officer?

Len waited two days, until Thursday, the night when the weekly poker game was played in the garage of Sam Hench's Studebaker dealership. The game was not secret; in fact, on warm nights they left the heavy wooden garage doors open, and anyone who walked by the establishment late at night could look in and see six or seven men sitting under a wire-covered work light, the fog of tobacco smoke keeping the mosquitoes away. The garage had become the regular site for the game because it was always available, because the players could dump their ashes and crush out their smokes right on the oil-stained concrete floor, and because it was right across the street from Staples' Bar—On and Off Sale. Sam Hench threw a heavy canvas tarp over a table brought out from the showroom, the players pulled up mismatched chairs and stools, the chips, stamped with the letters B.P.O.E. because they once belonged to an Elks Club in another city, were allotted, and the cards were dealt.

Len himself played a few years back, but he soon quit. If he drank during the game he lost money; he couldn't keep track of the cards or the betting. If he didn't drink, the frustration of being in the presence of liquor but not imbibing made it difficult for him to concentrate and he lost anyway. Nevertheless Len knew who was in the game, and from the first week Bennett came to town, he had been sitting in.

Shortly after eleven o'clock, the hour when Bentrock's streets were generally empty and its houses dark, but when the poker game was still in its early stages, Len entered the Northern Pacific Hotel. He did not go in through the heavy glass door that opened on the lobby. He climbed the fire escape and crawled through an unlatched window at the south end of the second floor.

Len remained right by the window, at the darkened end of the hall, close to a set of floor-length curtains he could step behind if it became necessary. From there Len could see the length of the hall, all the way to Room 202, the room that Bennett occupied. The night was warm, and no air moved in the hallway, but Len did not remove his coat. The pistol rested heavily in the coat's right-hand pocket, and he did not want to separate himself from it.

While he waited, Len let his thoughts rest on Gail Hayden. He was a realistic man; he knew that such a clear-eyed, lovely young woman was not likely to regard him as anything but what he was—a hawk-faced, stoop-shouldered drunk, old enough to be her father. That was all right. Even in his untethered dreams he came no closer than a father. He liked to imagine her walking down a street, day or night, and he kept pace with her, staying just a yard or two behind. Occasionally she would look back and smile, content that he was there to protect her. He was not well traveled; he had never been further from Montana's borders than North Dakota, but he played out his little scene in different locations. He knew San Francisco was famous for its hilly streets, so he imagined the two of them walking up and down those steep grades. Daisy had once visited a cousin in Salt Lake City, and she brought back a postcard of the Great Salt Lake, which she had waded in. Len thought of Gail walking along that beach, with his footsteps denting the sand right behind hers. He wanted to travel even farther with this fantasy—to England or France perhaps—but he didn't know what their streets or countryside looked like, so he couldn't allow Gail to go there.

He wished he could walk right now. His lower back and legs ached from standing in one place for so long, but he bore the pain by telling himself that he was doing his duty, a job that struck him as so necessary he wondered why the hall was not lined with men willing to do it.

It was close to 2:00 A.M. when Bennett returned to his room, and even after he unlocked his door and went in, Len remained in place, according to his plan.

Within five minutes, Bennett came out again, wearing only an undershirt and trousers and carrying a towel. He was barefoot, but he stepped down with such force that Len could hear the muffled *thump* of Bennett's heels striking the carpet.

Only after Bennett went into the bathroom and closed the door behind him did Len McAuley leave his station. He walked quickly down the hall to Bennett's room, opened the door just wide enough to slip through, and went in.

A light was on beside the bed, a lamp with a white globe shade painted with pink flowers. Its soft light, combined with the fact that the bed's white chenille spread was carefully turned down on a precise diagonal, made Len wonder for a moment if he was in the right room. No, Bennett's scent was in the air—his hair oil, his cigar smoke, his beery breath. Len stepped into the closet and pulled the door shut.

As he stood in that black airless space he caught another odor that at first he could not place. Then it came to him: it was the smell of sweat and shoe leather—Bennett's feet stank, and his shoes were in the closet. Len almost pitied the man: all that cockiness and then feet that smelled like that. . . .

When he returned to his room, Bennett was whistling, a succession of notes that sounded more like a musician practicing his scales than any attempt to reproduce a tune. Then the whistles stopped and the notes were replaced by the high whining notes of the bedsprings.

Len heard the soft click of the lamp switch, and the thin strip of yellow light at his feet vanished. The total darkness made it seem to Len that his own breathing became more audible, and he drew shallower breaths.

Len counted slowly to one hundred. When he reached that number and realized he wasn't quite ready, he started over, this time pausing long enough between each number to let his fingers rise and fall at his sides. Finally he could put it off no longer, and he stepped from the closet.

From the unshaded window and the open transom came enough light for him to see that Bennett's sleeping head was turned in Len's direction.

He had waited all that time, yet Bennett's being asleep was something Len had not accounted for. He had only planned this far: He would step from the closet and. . . .

Bennett would say something, and Len would answer. Or Bennett would act, and Len would react. Now, however, it was all up to Len, and he didn't know what to do.

He brought the pistol out of his jacket pocket, the sight on the long barrel catching for a moment on a loose thread. Once the gun was in his hand, Len knew—as if the knowledge could not have come from thought but only from touch, from the pistol's weight, the handle's smooth wood—he would not use it. He let it hang at his side as though it was nothing but a piece of rusting iron he was carrying until he could find a suitable scrap heap.

Although he had no intention of using it, Len still pulled the hammer back. He hoped that cocking the old .44—a noise as loud as a hen's cluck—would wake Bennett and his eyes would open to an armed man in his room.

But Bennett did not stir. Len noticed how, in sleep, Bennett's features bunched and softened. It was hard to believe that this sleeper with his lips hanging open in a thick dumb pout was the same man who swaggered the streets of Bentrock.

Len cleared his throat. Bennett did not move. With as much voice as he could muster, Len said, "Mister. You, mister." Still nothing.

He lowered the hammer, and as he did he wondered if the hammer came down on an empty chamber. He had never even checked to see if the gun was loaded. Not that it mattered now. He slipped the revolver back into the pocket where it had rested so long its weight had a familiar feel.

Before he left Bennett's room, Len took a last look around. On the top of the bureau were some of the man's possessions and toiletries—a brush and comb, a bottle of hair tonic, a jackknife, a fountain pen, a tie clip, a wallet, and a few coins. Len pulled the stopper from the hair tonic and laid the bottle on its side, letting the oily liquid pour out and soak the lace runner covering the top of the dresser.

Len returned home just before dawn. He was not so drunk that he couldn't pause for a moment outside his back door and listen to his favorite birds. Somewhere up there in the branches crowding the eaves, mourning doves were cooing their questions at the lightening sky. He couldn't see them, but their call always seemed to come from another place, echoes without a source.

Daisy had baked a pie, and it sat in the center of the kitchen table. Her note said, "Made your favorite," which meant the pie was rhubarb. He cut a generous slice and lifted it carefully to the plate, performing the motion in the slow and deliberate way that he habitually used so his hands would not give away his condition.

Before he ate, Len went to the sink to wash his hands one more time. When he spilled Bennett's hair tonic he got some of the oil on his hands, and he could not get rid of the heavy, sweet smell. Over at the jail he had scoured his hands with the lye soap they used for disinfecting certain prisoners. His hands were red from scrubbing, yet the odor remained. He did not want to lift a forkful of Daisy's pie to his mouth and smell Bennett's hair.

In a small dish beside the kitchen sink Daisy kept the chips and slivers of bar soap that were too small to be of use in the bath but which she could not bring herself to throw away. Len kept picking up piece after piece of soap, scrubbing frantically until the fragments melted or slipped away in his furious lathering. Neither could he wash away this drunken thought: what if someone smelled Bennett's scent on Len's hand—they might think he had his hand on the southerner's head.

When Gail Hayden crossed the street from her house to her office in the Mercer County Courthouse, Len McAuley was not at his window watching her. He was passed out at the kitchen table, his cheek pressed against the oilcloth. His hand rested between the upper and lower crusts of a wedge of pie, exactly where he had thrust it in the hope that the odor of sweetened, spiced, baked rhubarb would replace the smell of Pinaud's Hair Tonic.

The Sheriff's Wife
(1937)

❀ ❀ ❀

GAIL Hayden finally allowed the thought that she had pushed away for months to take hold: perhaps she had made a mistake in marrying this man.

She was sitting in a car parked along U.S. Highway Three ten miles outside Bentrock, Montana. It was January 1937, and in the past two days fifteen inches of snow had fallen in their part of the state. After the snow had stopped, she had ridden with her husband, the sheriff of Mercer County, out here to investigate a report of motorists stranded on the highway. They had followed behind the snowplow as it scraped away a single lane of traffic. The snow on either side of the highway was piled so high it felt as if they were driving through a tunnel of white walls. Then the road would take a turn, the wind couldn't find a place to stack the snow, and they would be out in the open, the highway so bare it looked as if it had been scoured clean.

She watched her husband walk toward the car in the ditch. He was wearing the huge buffalo coat that his father had given him. God, how she hated that coat! It stank so bad she made him hang it in the garage, and every time she went out there, it startled her, hanging on the wall like a great beast poised to leap at her.

He had insisted that she remain behind, not knowing what he might find in the car in the ditch. It could be a family, every one of them frozen to death. Or perhaps it was only the driver, a salesman who was caught in the storm and ran the heater as long as he could to keep warm while the snow drifted higher and higher, covering the car's tailpipe until carbon monoxide backed up into the car.

But if she was supposed to wait in the car, why had he asked her to come with him? It wasn't what she expected of him. He only asked her to accompany him on official duties when he was chaperoning dances out in the country—occasions that were more fun than work. Otherwise he kept the details of his work from her, even when she wished he'd share them with her.

Last summer, for example, when everyone in town was buzzing about the double murder out at the Gardner farm—Mr. and Mrs. Gardner killed in their bed by someone with an axe—he had known all along that it was Bobby Gardner, that pathetic fat boy who had been hearing voices, the voices, he said, of gangsters in Chicago, telling him to kill his parents. Bobby was arrested, tried, and hustled off to the state mental hospital before anyone in town had time to stir up any outrage that he was not put to death or imprisoned for life.

Or last fall when someone was killed out on the Soo Line tracks, and the newspaper said the body couldn't be identified. "Who do you suppose it could be?" she asked a few days after the accident. "It was Randall Loves Bear," he said quietly. Alongside the tracks he had found the burlap sack that Randall always carried, filled with scraps of food, old magazines and

186

newspapers, and empty whiskey bottles. Her husband wouldn't release the information until Randall's family was notified.

And when he took that length of iron pipe from the basement he let her believe that he was going to help someone with their plumbing, but in fact he was going out to the Bliss farm to arrest Clarence Bliss for stealing feed from his neighbors. Clarence was a big man, known for his quick temper, and he had been arrested on two other occasions for brawling. Wesley brought the pipe for protection.

Perhaps he needed her now to help carry someone from the car, someone frozen too stiff—dead or alive—for one person to manage. But why her? Why hadn't he brought Len McAuley, his deputy, or one of those men who was always hanging around the jail or the courthouse?

Was there something he wanted her to see? To know? Was there something about him that she couldn't understand until she saw him immediately after he had looked at a dead body? Did he want her to see one too—was that the only way they could finally be one, as a husband and wife were supposed to be?

If that was true, she wasn't sure, she just wasn't sure. . . .

He had not been a sheriff when they met. Then he had been Wesley Hayden, student of law at the University of North Dakota, and she had been the secretary at Kramer's Chiropractic Clinic, where he came for treatment for his bad

187

back. The way he limped when he walked in, even she knew his problem wasn't his back; it was his bad leg. After he had come in a few times, she finally asked what had happened to his leg.

"A horse kicked me," he answered. "Broke my knee like it was a dish plate."

"I bet that's your problem," she said. "Not your back. The way you walk twists your spine."

He smiled for the first time in all his visits. "I thought you were the secretary."

"It's just common sense," she said.

"Maybe if I had talked to you earlier I could have saved myself some money."

She shrugged modestly, but that was exactly what she had been thinking.

He kept on coming to the clinic, though she wasn't sure whether he came because Dr. Kramer was actually helping him or to see her. Finally he said he wanted to ask her out on a date but not before she told him about herself. That made her angry—as if he didn't know her well enough already—but she looked him right in the eye and said she was Gail Berdahl, the only daughter of Carl and Anna Berdahl of Kettleton, North Dakota. Her parents owned a farm in the Red River valley, but she wanted to get away. Not only was she the first member of her family to graduate from high school, but she had gone on to secretarial school as well. She had been working for Dr. Kramer for a year and a half. She attended services every Sunday at Faith Lutheran Church, and taught Sunday School to first-graders. She smoked cigarettes, had nothing against dancing, and even took a drink of whiskey from time to time. And he, she said, reminded her of every university student she had met—so full of himself it was leaking out the top. If he hadn't blushed, she probably would not have gone out with him. She certainly wouldn't have fallen in love with him.

They were married as soon as he finished law school, and their plan was to move to his hometown of Bentrock, in northeastern Montana. His father had indicated that he could guide some business his son's way and help him get his law practice off the ground. That was all Wesley needed to hear. He decided that it was important to him, after all, to return to the place he came from. Gail simply wanted to see more of the world, even if it was another part of the Great Plains, a small town in Montana.

At first things worked out according to their design. They lived in a small apartment above a bar, and though their place smelled of stale beer and cigar smoke, they suffered through it without complaint because Wesley's father owned the building, and they were able to live there rent-free. In spite of his father's promises, Wesley's practice didn't earn much money initially—he was as likely to be paid with canned goods, homegrown vegetables, or a newly slaughtered chicken as with money—but Gail said nothing. She knew how important it was for him to acquire clients, whether they could pay or not. And one woman was so grateful for Wesley's handling of her husband's estate that she gave them a hand-sewn quilt that kept them warm through their first winter. Besides, Gail had been able to find work as a secretary in the Register of Deeds office. They weren't rich, but they weren't poor either, and they knew their livelihood would improve.

In fact, Gail was surprised to find out how much she loved Montana. Her infatuation began the day of her very first visit when they drove toward Bentrock at the end of the day, just as the sun was setting over the prairie. The colors! Pinks fading into shades of purple, violet, and lavender—all merging into deep blue. She had seen sunsets before. What she had never seen, since she came from a region that was flat as a tabletop, was the way those colors crept out of the hollows of the darkening hills and the hues of the land seemed to match the sky.

She grew to love the hills too, the way some of them were nothing more than a gradual swell of grassland, as if the earth was simply drawing a breath, and then others were sudden eruptions, rocks breaking angrily through the prairie.

Just east of Bentrock was a hill she liked to climb, and from its height she could look down at the town, the straight lines and right angles of telephone wires and streets interrupted by intermittent bursts of trees in leaf. My town, she would say to herself; this is the town where I will make my life.

True, it was not as prosperous as the communities in her native Red River valley, but the people were for the most part like the people she had grown up around, simple, hardworking, quiet, God-fearing—Swedes and Norwegians mostly, just as in her home county, though here there were a few more Germans and Russians. And Indians. Mercer County was next to the Fort Murdoch Reservation, and its residents, Blackfeet mostly as well as a few Cheyenne and Chippewa, often came into Bentrock. Some Bentrock residents, her brother-in-law especially, tried to frighten her with stories about wild drunken Indians, but Gail saw the truth. When they came to town they tried hard not to be noticed. In this way they were no different than those solitary ranchers and sheepherders from the outlying regions who, when they had to come to town, acted as though they were in a foreign country and wanted to get back home as quickly as possible.

Gail also made friends soon after moving to Bentrock. The woman who worked right across the hall from her in the courthouse was only a year older than Gail. This woman—Beverly Hilland—was from Alabama and absolutely confounded by her new state and its residents. As Gail tried to explain the ways of these northern plains people to Beverly, Gail came to feel as though she was something of a native herself.

She also made friends with Daisy McAuley, an older woman who was the deputy sheriff's wife. Daisy lived right across the street from the jail and the courthouse, and she often came over to have coffee with Gail and Beverly. Daisy always brought something freshly baked—cinnamon rolls or cookies or coffee cake—and with the pastries she also brought whispered tales about whose farm or business was going to be foreclosed upon, who was planning to go to Great Falls to have her gall bladder removed, or who was having trouble controlling his drinking. Between Daisy's gossip and Wesley's stories about his clients, Gail soon felt as though she knew as much about Bentrock and its citizens as people who had lived there all their lives.

She had no doubt that she and Wesley would live the rest

of their lives in Bentrock, and that fact did not disturb her in the least. She knew who and what she was—a small-town girl with simple tastes and modest ambitions. If she could move into a house large enough to raise a family in, she would be happy.

Then something happened that threatened to change everything.

Julian Hayden, the sheriff and her father-in-law, decided that his son should succeed him in office. Julian's plan was that Wesley would hold the post for a term, and then Julian or Len McCauley would take over again. There was no question that Wesley would be elected; the Hayden name carried more weight than any other in the county, and the last two times Julian ran for office he didn't even have an opponent.

And there was no question that Wesley would do what his father asked. Wesley and his brother were not simply polite and obedient where their father was concerned; they were completely submissive, just as their mother was. Enid Hayden was a meek, high-strung woman for whom even normal conversation required great effort. "Enid's nerves are bad," people said. Even the simple acts of day-to-day living, such as preparing a meal or going to the store or arranging a visit to the hairdresser, often seemed too much for her. Gail knew Enid was like that at least in part because she was married to Julian Hayden. Julian so completely dominated and browbeat his wife that at the sound of his voice she jumped as if a door had slammed. And when Mrs. Hayden entered a room, Wesley and his brother didn't even look up; when their father entered they automatically fell silent and often stood. Where

Gail was from it was understood that children would behave respectfully toward their parents, but this went beyond anything she had seen. The way the boys behaved around their father reminded her of the way some Catholics in her hometown acted toward the old priest.

The simple fact of Wesley being sheriff—that didn't concern Gail. She feared that once he put on that badge he would become like his father.

She treated Julian Hayden politely—she didn't know any other way—but she could never like the man, never, never. He was everything she was brought up to believe a man should not be. He bullied his wife and sons and anyone who showed him deference. He talked too loud and he cursed in the presence of women. He was arrogant. When he showed generosity toward others he made certain it became known. He flattered and he boasted. Worst of all, he was charming. And he knew it.

Shortly after she came to Bentrock, Gail witnessed a scene that revealed Julian Hayden both as a man and as a law officer.

Around noon one day her father-in-law appeared out in front of the jail with a prisoner in tow. The prisoner was a tall, shabbily dressed man who was so thin it looked as though he might literally be starving. Julian brought this prisoner out by the collar and proceeded to haul the man down the steps of the courthouse. Right out there where everyone could see, the sheriff marched the man the few blocks to the center of town. The sight was so unusual that townspeople came out from their homes and businesses and followed Julian Hayden down the street. Gail and Beverly went along with everyone else. The little parade finally stopped at the train depot, where the 12:20 train was loading and would soon leave for Havre, Shelby, Cut Bank, and points west.

There, in front of all those witnesses, Julian Hayden bought his prisoner a one-way ticket to Spokane. The sheriff almost lifted the man onto the train, and once he was on, Julian said to him, in a voice so loud everyone could hear, "And if you come back here and try to pull any of those shenanigans again I'll do worse than boot your ass out of town. We don't need your kind around here." The train began to pull out, and as it did, Julian reached into his coat pocket and brought out a revolver. He held it aloft and shouted again at the man on the train (though perhaps the man could no longer hear him): "And don't be getting any ideas about coming back for this. You'll play hell trying to get it back from me."

The entire scene was so dramatic that a few people actually applauded their sheriff. Julian, however, gave no sign of having noticed the crowd. He pushed past the bystanders and their questions about what the man had done and how the sheriff had caught him, and walked directly back to the courthouse.

That night Gail told Wesley what she had seen his father do. As she finished her story Wesley began to laugh.

"What's so funny?" she asked.

"Dad," he said, shaking his head.

"What? What did he do?"

"That 'criminal' he put on the train was nothing but an old bum who came into the jail the night before last, drunk and with no place to stay. I know, I was there when he came in. He asked Dad if he could sleep the night in the jail. Now he's Spokane's problem."

"Why did your father send him there?"

"Damned if I know. Maybe he's got family there. Wouldn't be the first time Dad has reached into his own pocket to buy someone a ticket home."

Gail thought she already knew the answer to her next question, but she asked anyway. "What about the gun?"

Wesley shrugged. "Probably some rusty old pistol Dad had lying around the office."

It was clear to Gail that Wesley admired his father for what he had done, for his generosity as well as his cleverness and his showmanship, but for her part Gail felt ashamed that she had even been on the street during her father-in-law's little show.

Right after the election, Julian resigned so Wesley could take over right away. Julian and his wife moved out of their house across from the courthouse and back to the family ranch. Wesley and Gail were to move into the vacant house, a two-story white frame house with a huge backyard. The house was lovely—spacious and clean and newly painted inside and out—and to go to work all she had to do was walk across the street. Nevertheless, she did not feel right about the house. Moving into it meant taking one more step away from their own lives.

She tried to talk herself out of her concerns. Wesley was

nothing like his father. Not at all. He was a gentle, thoughtful, soft-spoken and soft-hearted man whose main goal in life— and in this he was completely unlike his father—was not to be noticed. Campaigning for office, what little of it he had to do, had been difficult for him. Every time he had to make a speech before any group—the Farmers Union or the Ladies Auxiliary —she could see how tense he became, how the knots around his jaw tightened and the lines above his brow deepened. No, he was not his father.

Then one day in early December Gail had occasion to leave her desk and go down to the sheriff's office in the basement of the courthouse. She wanted to ask Wesley if he would be free that evening so they could go bowling with Beverly and her husband.

Wesley was at his desk. His desk? It was the same rolltop desk that Julian had sat at for so many years. The same leather-bound law books were lined on top of the desk. The same railroad calendar hung over the books. The odor of Julian's cigars lingered in the air. But that was her husband sitting there.

She said his name and he turned toward her, tilting back in his chair just as his father had always done.

He was wearing his hat. Wesley never wore his hat indoors. But his father did.

One detail unsettled Gail even more than the hat. When her husband faced her, she noticed his badge. How could she have missed this before?

He did not have his badge pinned to his coat. Instead, he had it hooked and hanging from the pocket of his vest, the pin

196

inside, the shield outside. Exactly the way his father wore his badge. The same badge.

For a moment she couldn't speak. Had she taken a wrong turn somewhere—gone left instead of right at the bottom of those narrow stairs?

"What is it, Gail?" Wesley asked. "Is there something wrong?"

She shook her head, as much to clear her mind as to answer him. She finally stammered out what she had come to ask him. "Do you want . . . will you be available to go bowling tonight with Bev and Mitch?"

"That sounds fine," he said. "I should be done here around six." Then, while she still stood in the doorway, he turned back to his desk.

Although the snow had stopped hours earlier, out here in the country the wind stirred it up in such thick swirls and gusts it might as well still be falling. Wesley had left the car running but the heater could not compete with the cold, and the windows were beginning to frost over. Gail squinted hard in Wesley's direction. What if she did not know that was him, she thought. Would she be able to tell? He was wearing his father's coat and doing his father's job. Was there anything to tell her with certainty that the man standing up to his knees in snow, peering into a parked car and trying its doors, was her husband?

He started back toward her, his head tilted to avoid the

wind's icy sting. The limp! Of course! That listing walk could belong only to Wesley. As he approached the car, she reached over and opened his door.

He shivered with cold as he situated himself behind the wheel. "By God, that wind is something," he said. Gail watched the flakes of snow on his coat melt to droplets of water.

"Is anyone in there?" she asked.

He shook his head. "Must have tried walking. I can't see any sign of tracks, so maybe they got somewhere before the storm hit full force. If they didn't. . . ." He didn't have to finish the sentence. Everyone knew what happened if you were caught out in the open in a blizzard. Every landmark would vanish, and without anything to give you your bearings you could walk in circles before freezing to death. Everyone in the state knew how easily it could happen, and if their memories were short, every winter they got a reminder: someone died in the snow.

"Maybe someone picked them up," Gail suggested.

"Maybe."

His hands gripped the steering wheel, but Wesley made no move to drive away. He's probably waiting to thaw out a little, Gail thought. No matter what the reason, she was going to take advantage of this moment when she had him alone.

"Wesley, can I ask you something?"

He had taken off his gloves and was breathing on his fingers to warm them up. Years ago he had been pheasant hunting in the fall when the weather turned suddenly cold, and he had to walk miles back to his car. He wasn't dressed for the weather, and his hands had been so cold he thought he might have gotten a touch of frostbite. Since then his hands were always cold, no matter what the temperature.

"Uh-huh," he answered absently. He clenched and unclenched his fists. "I should have worn mittens. Gloves don't keep your hands warm worth a damn."

"Why did you bring me out here?"

He looked at her as though he didn't understand her question. "Why?" he repeated.

"Yes, why. Was there something you wanted me to see? There's nothing out here but snow."

He continued to stare at her with an expression that was half bewilderment and half consternation.

"Did your father ever take your mother out on a call like this?"

He was more confused than ever, but she could see that he was getting angry too. The mention of his father had done that.

"Never," he answered.

"Are you sure? Perhaps many years ago, before your memory." Gail had held the theory that Julian Hayden had somehow broken his wife, broken her the way a cowboy broke a horse, and maybe this was how he had done it, by bringing her along on a mission like this. And once she had seen what he saw regularly in his line of work—the exploded body of a man hit by a freight train, the blackened eyes of a woman beaten by her husband, the tears of a boy who knows that once the pickup is lifted off him, his legs will be gone—he thought that she'd be docile forever, forever fearful that he would show her again what kinds of horrors the world routinely offers.

"I thought," he said, his voice lowering and taking on the slow cadence that he affected when he was trying to hold his temper, "that you might like to get out. You've been cooped up for a couple days with this storm. That's all. Don't make so much of things."

Was he telling the truth? She couldn't tell. He seemed sincere, innocent in his intentions, but she simply didn't know. The man she married had become unreadable.

He shook his head and reached for the gearshift. Whenever he couldn't understand her, he always made it seem as though there was something wrong with *her*. What's more, he often implied that it had to do somehow with the way she was raised, the region, the people she was from, as much to say, here we don't think such thoughts; in my family we don't act that way.

But she was not finished. She had been playing with an idea for weeks, since before Christmas. It was a reckless notion, she knew, but as she had watched the changes in Wesley, she had become desperate.

She put her gloved hand on his and stopped him from putting the car in gear. "Wait," she said.

He didn't look at her or move his hand from under hers.

"I want to tell you something." She took her hand away and pulled the collar of her coat tighter. "We're. . . . I'm, I'm expecting."

Now he looked at her blankly, as if he was waiting for her to finish her sentence. Expecting? Expecting what? Whom?

It was a lie, but that was what she had come to. She couldn't think of any other way to pry her husband loose from his job, his father. Perhaps if another life were involved she could persuade Wesley that this wild country—where you could perish in your car on a winter's day—was no place for their son or daughter to grow up.

Yet now that her plan was out in the open it seemed as insubstantial as a snowflake. How would this revelation change anything? What could she have been thinking?

At first he said nothing, then he reached for her and held her in an awkward embrace. Their heavy coats, the close quarters of the car's front seat—it was all they could do to lean their weight into one another, and because of the cold they had to avoid touching any exposed flesh.

When he finally spoke his voice sounded thick, as though his throat was clotted with snow. "Another generation," he said, "another generation born in Mercer County."

Over Wesley's shoulder Gail looked out across the road. The wind carried a plume of snow off the top of the drift, and it looked as if the snow was smoking. The wind carved the edge of the drift as sharp as a knife's blade.

On September 13, 1937, almost nine months exactly after the January day when Gail made that false announcement to her husband, their son was born in the Good Samaritan Hospital in Dixon, Montana, a town forty miles from Bentrock, which had no hospital of its own.

201

They named their son after her father, Carl David Hayden, but decided they would call him David. Gail always thought that David, and her pregnancy with him, was responsible for saving her marriage.

Shortly after the long labor and difficult delivery, Wesley cautiously entered the hospital room where his wife lay. He wore the expression that all new fathers wear, half joy and half shame for what their wives endured.

He sat tentatively on the side of the bed, as if his full weight might spill his exhausted wife from the mattress.

"Did you see him?" she asked.

He nodded, and grinning inanely said, "He's the biggest baby in there." Gail knew their son had barely weighed seven pounds.

A nurse came in and gave Gail a hypodermic to help her sleep. Before she lost consciousness entirely, she heard Wesley speak to the nurse. Gail couldn't be sure—had he said, "It looks like Mercer County is going to have another Hayden for sheriff"?

The Visit
(1937)

❀ ❀ ❀

GAIL Hayden closed her eyes and listened for her father downstairs. He was always up before dawn, lighting the stove, putting water on to boil, making coffee, dressing to go out to begin his chores. Gail's mother would shortly follow her husband downstairs. Her mother's one indulgence was to wait until the kitchen warmed up before she got out of bed.

But Gail couldn't hear her father yet. She opened her eyes and tried to guess how far off dawn was without looking at the clock. She looked through the gap left by the partially pulled-down window shade. The darkness seemed to be losing its strength, as if it were a softening shadow and not an unwavering blank of blackness, as moonless nights often were in the country. She shut her eyes once more.

It was a November morning like so many other November mornings when Gail had awakened in this room. Outside the ground would be iron gray with frost or a mottled white from a scattering of snow. The cats would be leaving the barn and making for the kitchen's warmth. Soon her mother would call up the stairs telling Gail it was time to get ready for school. . . .

But it was November, 1937. Gail had been out of school for close to ten years, and it had been almost that long since

Gail lived in this house, on this farm in North Dakota's Red River valley. Her home now was in northeastern Montana, in Bentrock, the county seat of Mercer County, where her husband was the sheriff. Where the barren rocky soil had a reddish cast that always made her think that the land had once been on fire.

She had left her husband to come back home. No, no, that wasn't the way to say it. It was the baby. Yes, she had left her husband, but he wanted her to go. No, he hadn't sent her away. It was the baby, the baby.

Gail opened her eyes to slow her whirling thoughts. She turned her gaze to the bassinet at the other side of the room where her sleeping baby lay. Even in the early morning darkness the bassinet, with its covering of white cloth and lace, glowed like no other object in the room. Where did it find light to reflect back to her eyes, she wondered?

She listened for her son's breathing. Could she hear it? She wasn't sure, but something, some disturbance of air seemed to be in the room with her. She almost believed the bedroom was warmer—by a degree? half a degree?—from her baby's presence, from the heat emanating from his tightly wrapped body, from the tiny chuffs of breath he sent into the air. She was often surprised, when she picked him up, by how warm he was, how he seemed at times to be nothing more than a miniature engine for producing heat.

She listened too for the murmuring smacking sounds he would make just before he began to cry to be fed. She could feel it was almost time. Her baby's hunger registered in her body just as it did in his. His emptiness. Her fullness. His need. Her ache. Soon they would relieve each other.

She shifted onto her side, a position that increased the discomfort in her swollen breasts. Once when Gail was a young girl and visiting her cousins' farm near McKenzie, North Dakota, she sprained her ankle. She and her cousins had been playing Red Rover, Gail had been running, and she stepped in a gopher hole, twisting her ankle so sharply she was surprised it didn't break. "Just a bad sprain," the doctor said as he probed and gently manipulated the foot. Her ankle swelled to twice its normal size, and despite the tightness and pain, Gail could not resist moving her foot. The way, since the baby, she could not resist pressing gently against her milk-heavy breasts. The ache was there—steady and dull—but she could tolerate it.

Her son was the reason for this visit. She had brought her first-born child here for her parents to see, to show her son— to show David—off to all the uncles and aunts, the cousins, the old friends and acquaintances who still lived in North Dakota. The trip had been at least in part her husband Wesley's idea. "If you go to them," he said, "rather than wait for them to come to Montana, you'll be able to make this a vacation. Your mother will do the cooking and cleaning, and you can relax and take care of the baby. Stay as long as you like. Get good and rested before you come home."

Gail left, then, of her own accord. She was not sent away. When Wesley put her and the baby on the train, he kissed her and told her he would miss her while she was away.

So she did not leave her husband in the way that some of the town's gossips—in both Montana and North Dakota— might whisper and speculate about. Gail would make her visit, she would let her parents coo and cluck over this beautiful baby, she would let them wait on her until this fatigue—which made her feel, *after* the baby was born, as if she were carrying extra weight, as if every bone in her body had somehow been transformed to heavy iron—finally lifted, and then she would go back to Montana, back to her home and back to her husband.

Why then, from the moment she first entered this house of her childhood, did this thought wrap itself around her: I do not have to leave here, not ever again. She stepped into the parlor and saw her mother's doilies pinned carefully to the backs and arms of every chair, she breathed in that familiar household aroma—a mixture, it seemed to her, of baking bread and furniture wax—she heard the furnace clunk and gasp before it began to blow out hot air, and she thought—God help her, she could not keep from thinking—she would never have to set foot in Montana again.

She tried to shake loose the thought immediately, to toss it off like a heavy blanket on a warm night, but she could not get free of it. Its weight and comfort was too much for her.

When her mother held a jar of applesauce under hot water to loosen the lid, when her father looked into his coffee cup, then swirled the dregs before swallowing, when Gail lay her baby on the bed in the very same depression in the mattress that Gail's own weight had made, every time some little familiarity struck her, she thought—again and again and again—this was once my home. And it could be again.

There was nothing extraordinary in any of these moments or in any of these sights, but their very ordinariness was their appeal. Because Gail could not eliminate from her memory the picture of something quite extraordinary. And Wesley was in the center of this picture, exactly where she wished he would not be. . . .

The previous spring, on the first weekend in May, on a Saturday evening when, long after the sun had set, the air was still soft and warm as it can be only on nights in May. The previous winter had been particularly long and hard, even for northeastern Montana. They got their first heavy snow in late October, and from then until the end of April the snow cover was continuous. Usually an excess of snow meant, as Wesley and the other natives of the region told her, milder temperatures, but last winter that had not been true. December, January, February—all saw record-breaking cold. And still the snows came.

A part of Gail wanted to blame the weather, to say that people had been cooped up too long, that when they were finally released into the warm spring air, when they finally got to stand with their feet on dry earth—not in snow or mud—it was too much for them. In their giddy joy they dropped some of the restraints and inhibitions that they would usually hold tight to.

That was what one part of her said. Another said, what could you expect—this was Montana, the West, and that it was once called Wild was a source of pride for many of its citizens. Why, if the people in the part of North Dakota where Gail grew up knew that *their* region was called wild, they would hang their heads in shame. Or try to do something about it.

209

Oh, Gail told herself so many things—the weather was to blame. The state itself. Her father-in-law. The badge. The situation. The Indian. Anything to avoid saying: Wesley. His nature.

They hadn't been at the dance from its start. Wesley wanted to make his rounds in town first and then finish up the night at the small country tavern where all the tables had been taken outdoors to make room inside for dancing and the music makers—an accordionist, a fiddle player, and a drummer.

By the time Gail and Wesley arrived, there were as many people outside as in. The tavern was small anyway, and all the bodies—warmed by the day's heat and the night's dancing—made it impossibly stuffy. Besides, the night was clear and pleasant, why not stand outside with a whiskey or a beer in hand, stare up at the stars, and sigh once more to anyone who would listen, "My God, wasn't this winter a long one."

Wesley did not expect trouble at this dance; he was simply putting in an appearance, showing himself in order to say, "There is law in Mercer County, Montana." This strategy he learned from his father, who held the office before Wesley. "Keep moving," his father often advised. "Let 'em know you're around. A minute here. A minute there. They'll never know where you're going to show up next." But this dance was the last planned stop on the nightly tour; Wesley could allow himself a drink now, and he led Gail to the bar.

He ordered a whiskey and ginger ale for Gail and a glass of beer for himself. Paul Gurch, the tavern owner, served them. As he set the drinks down, he said to Wesley, "You think that's a problem down there?" He nodded toward the end of

210

the bar where an Indian sat drinking alone.

The Indian looked familiar to Gail, but she could not be sure where she had seen him. Perhaps he was simply a town Indian, as those who did not live on the nearby reservation were called. Though he was sitting on a bar stool and hunched over his drink, Gail could tell he was a large man. He wore overalls dark with grease and dirt, and under the overalls was an equally dirty flannel shirt, so old the plaid had worn almost to invisibility. He had long hair, uncombed and hanging down his back in oily strands.

Wesley took one look at the Indian and shook his head with the kind of mild disgust he usually reserved for machines that did not work properly. "LaChapelle," Wesley said.

Then Gail knew. It was Gordon LaChapelle, known throughout the region, in the towns and on the reservation, as no good, a troublemaker, a rough customer. He was a bootlegger, a car thief, and, rumor had it, a killer. He had done time in the state penitentiary for armed robbery and for assault and battery. Wesley had arrested him a few times but never for anything more serious than public drunkenness and brawling. He was, she had heard more than one person say, a bad Indian. Her father-in-law had once said, "Mercer County would be better off if someone would come up behind LaChapelle and put a bullet in his brain."

Wesley quietly asked Paul Gurch, "Has he said anything? Done anything?"

"Just sitting there drinking. Drinking a lot."

"You could stop serving him."

"How do you suppose he'd take to that?"

211

Wesley shrugged. "Is Len here?"

"Haven't seen him."

Wesley looked slowly around the the bar as if he were counting the house. To Gail he said through a forced smile, "Why don't you sip your drink and I'll be right back."

As he moved down the bar toward LaChapelle, Gail wondered if it was his job or his knee that was paining him at that moment. She wanted to reach out to him, as she had wanted to on other occasions when she saw him off to do this work that was his duty. Stop, she wanted to say; don't go. This is your father's job, not yours. Leave this work to him and to others like him. Turn away, just turn away this time.

But Gail said nothing. Not any of the previous times and not tonight.

Wesley took a place at the bar next to Gordon LaChapelle, and though Wesley did not sit down, he leaned companionably against the bar, as though he had no other thought than to drink his beer and chat with the bar's patrons. Wesley was in shirtsleeves, and nothing identified him as the sheriff, but that didn't matter. Everyone in the county knew who he was and who his father was.

The music and din of the bar was too loud for Gail to hear what Wesley was saying. And perhaps LaChapelle didn't hear him either for he remained hunched over his drink. Wesley must have spoken again, because the Indian finally acknowledged the sheriff's presence.

Gordon LaChapelle slowly lifted his head and turned his broad, beefy face toward Wesley. The Indian's eyes were barely open, but he held his gaze steadily on Wesley.

Her husband kept talking, but LaChapelle never replied. He simply stared at Wesley, blinking slowly as if it was all he could do to keep himself awake on his bar stool. Gail still felt there was something dangerous about him, for all his languor. He reminded her of a cat who feigns disinterest before pouncing. Her husband was not carrying a weapon. Once more, she had the urge to call him away. At just that moment, however, he walked away from LaChapelle and came back to her.

He cocked his head toward his right shoulder in a gesture that had become familiar to Gail. She knew its meaning, too, even if her husband did not. It meant, I know I'm supposed to do something but damned if I know what.

Wesley set his glass on the bar. It was empty, and Gail could not remember seeing him lift it to his lips.

Paul Gurch swept the glass from the bar to refill it. "Well?" he asked Wesley.

"I guess he just wants to drink his whiskey."

"My whiskey. He's done that. When's he going to move on?" He placed the refilled glass in front of Wesley.

Wesley cocked his head again.

Paul Gurch gestured toward the crowd outside the bar. "There are people out there who'd like to come in here and dance. That's what this was supposed to be."

"What's stopping them?"

Paul Gurch made no move to look or point in Gordon LaChapelle's direction. "You know," he said in a lowered voice.

"You sure you haven't seen Len?"

"He hasn't come in."

Wesley pointed to Gail's drink. "How is that? About ready for another?"

She put her hand over the top of her glass. She knew he wasn't thinking about her drink. "I'm fine," she answered.

"Sure?" His smile made her nervous.

"I'm sure."

"Could you do me a favor then? Could you go outside and ask Jack Pepper to come in?" Jack Pepper was a hired hand on Julian Hayden's ranch. Gail had met him only once, but she knew she would have no trouble recognizing him. He was well over six feet tall, broad shouldered, and heavyset, and with a head so large that Gail wondered how he managed to find a hat that fit him. Wesley insisted that Jack Pepper was a good man, hardworking, reliable, and loyal to Wesley's father and the ranch, but Gail felt uneasy around him. He had a way, as some men did, of emphasizing his size around her and other women, done in a way calculated not to impress but to frighten her. Gail would do as Wesley asked, but she did not look forward to approaching Jack Pepper in the parking lot.

He was easy to find. He was wearing a white shirt, and on the moonlit night his broad back stood out like a ship's sail on the sea. He was standing with a group of men, all of them drinking and smoking. When Gail tapped Jack Pepper on the back, she interrupted a conversation about horses.

"Excuse me," she said as he turned around. "My husband would like to see you inside." Then it occurred to her that he might not know who she was, much less to whom she was married. "Wesley Hayden. I believe he needs your assistance."

Gail didn't show much in her fifth month—not much

more than a little tummy—but she had taken to wearing maternity clothes nonetheless. It was due to shyness more than anything else. She would let her appearance announce her condition to the town. If she looked pregnant, she wouldn't have to respond to every busybody's question about whether the rumor was true that she was expecting.

Perhaps the cotton print maternity smock she wore that night caused Jack Pepper to treat her with unusual respect. Or perhaps it was nothing so noble on his part. Perhaps he was simply obeying a command that came from Julian Hayden's son.

Jack Pepper set his bottle on the ground, tossed his cigarette away in a shower of sparks, and strode quickly toward the bar.

Gail wasn't sure what she should do. Wesley had told her to wait for him outside, but she couldn't stand there with that group of cowboys. She looked around the lot for someone she knew. She recognized faces but saw no one she would feel comfortable approaching. If there were a group of women she could stand with them, but all the women were with husbands or boyfriends. So Gail did what she was hoping to do all along—she walked back to the bar and looked through its smeared window to see what her husband and Jack Pepper were going to do.

What happened inside coincided so precisely with her arrival at the window that it seemed as though it were staged for her benefit.

Gail saw her husband walk behind Gordon LaChapelle. Wesley must have done so quietly because LaChapelle didn't turn on his stool to watch him. When Wesley was directly behind the Indian, he reached up and grabbed him by his hair, pulling LaChapelle backwards off his stool.

LaChapelle was caught completely off balance, and he fell so heavily that Gail wondered for an instant if his fall was caused by something else—could he have fainted and Wesley was only trying to catch him, to break his fall? No, if he had lost consciousness, he would have pitched forward, the way his weight was leaning. Besides, she could tell that Wesley had not just pulled LaChapelle back but had hurled the Indian to the floor.

The stool toppled over too, sliding out to the side while LaChapelle went straight back. The Indian cracked his head on the floor, and as soon as he hit, Jack Pepper—where had he come from?—grabbed one of his legs. Just as quickly, Wesley had the other leg, and together they dragged Gordon LaChapelle across the floor and toward the door.

At first Gail believed that LaChapelle must have been knocked unconscious by the fall, because he allowed himself to be dragged without protest. Then she saw his arm flop out to the side and his hand grab weakly for something to hold onto.

Wesley and Jack Pepper backed through the screen door, and as it closed behind them it banged against Gordon LaChapelle's ribs.

By now a crowd had gathered, and the people formed a kind of circle—half of them in the bar and half of them outside watching.

Once they were outside, Wesley nodded to indicate they

were to drag him to the right, in the opposite direction from where Gail stood. Wesley asked Jack Pepper, "Did he leave anything on the bar? Money? A hat?"

"I didn't see nothing."

Then they were out of sight, behind some parked cars and trucks. Gail knew she wouldn't follow them, no matter how badly she wanted to know what was going on, so she listened intently.

She heard some grunts, some breathy exhalations of air, some scuffling sounds—all of which could have come as easily from a man being beaten or a man being helped to his feet.

No one else in the crowd ventured behind the parked cars either, a fact that Gail considered remarkable considering these people's curiosity and their level of inebriation. If it were merely a fight they would have all gathered around—she had seen that often enough—but this was official business; since the sheriff was involved it was best to stay back.

Gail was still standing alone, and she could tell that others were staring at her. Because she was pregnant? Because she was the sheriff's wife? Her baby shifted inside her, a slow liquid roll that felt almost deliberate and made Gail feel as if she was nothing more than a vessel, as if this life inside her was as likely to respond to the moon's pull as to Gail's will.

A truck's engine coughed and sputtered to life, and then a nearby stand of birch trees was briefly illuminated by headlights sweeping past. Gail guessed that was Gordon LaChapelle driving away, and she wondered how far he'd get in his beaten, drunken condition. There were so many accidents along these county roads—someone missing a curve and rolling down a ravine, a car or truck stalling on the railroad tracks, a driver too drunk or sleepy to go on and pulling off on the shoulder only to be crashed into by another car. It distressed her that so many of these accidents involved Indians.

Wesley and Jack Pepper walked out from behind the parked cars. Wesley scuffed his feet through the gravel and thrust his hands deep into his trouser pockets as if embarrassed to be the focus of so much attention.

Gail heard Jack Pepper ask Wesley, "Where'd he get that truck?"

"I have no idea."

"I try to put a little money aside. I can't afford no new truck."

"You've got money saved?"

"I'm tryin'. I don't always manage."

"Tell my dad you need a raise."

"Your dad's always been fair with me. I got no kick."

Wesley saw Gail waiting for him and put his hand out to her as though he were meeting a prospective voter on the street. She took a step back.

"You want to go back inside?" he asked.

Jack Pepper drifted off to resume drinking with his friends. Gail could tell from the way they greeted him that they were eager to know what had happened with Gordon LaChapelle. She was, too, but she was in no hurry to ask Wesley.

"Are we staying?" she asked.

"We can go. I just have to talk to Paul Gurch for a moment."

"I'll wait out here."

"Suit yourself."

Wesley left her alone again. This time while she waited someone approached her. Carol Clifton, who also worked at the courthouse, walked unsteadily toward Gail. Carol looked like she was dressed for a square dance, in a bright yellow blouse and a wide flared skirt. Gail could see that Carol was drunk. She carried a bottle of beer, and she could not stop smiling at Gail.

"It's not like this, sweetie," Carol said.

"What isn't?"

"You know. Here. Living here."

"Just tonight?"

"Tonight, sure. I know you're thinking about your baby and all. I would, too. But I wouldn't worry. I mean, I don't."

"I was thinking about Wesley."

"Wes? He wears a tie." Carol pointed the neck of her beer bottle toward the group of cowboys. "That's who you should worry about. Donnie Eidsen over there? A steer stomped on his foot and it swelled up so bad he couldn't even pull on his boot, much less put it in a stirrup. So he ain't drawing his pay right now."

Gail squinted through the darkness. She wasn't sure who Donnie Eidsen was, but she thought she saw one of the cowboys leaning awkwardly against the hood of a car, and he may have been resting a sore foot on the car's bumper.

"Wes is workin' anyway," Carol said again.

"Yes, he is."

"Too bad he has to when you're around."

Wesley came out of the bar. He held the door open while he called something back to Paul Gurch. The open door let the bar's light tumble out and cast Wesley's silhouette on the ground. Gail kept her eye on the shadow, letting it tell her when her husband was coming her way.

Carol turned to leave, then stopped. "How much longer you going to work?"

Gail hunched her shoulders. "Until the doctor tells me I can't."

"See you Monday then!"

As they drove home Gail thought about how glad she was that she was pregnant. It meant Wesley would not initiate lovemaking that night. Since she announced her pregnancy he would not touch her in that way unless she indicated that it would be all right. And tonight she was not about to do that. She didn't want to take a chance that his blood might be heated not by desire for her but by the violent act he had been involved in. There had been times in the past when he came home late, after making an arrest, when he wanted her so badly it was all she could do to make him slow down. And she didn't mind giving herself to him if it meant their lovemaking could help wipe out some unpleasantness he had encountered on his job. But if he came to her simply because he was so full of himself he didn't know what else to do—why, then she didn't want him to touch her.

They had been in the car a long time, riding in silence, but

Gail knew Wesley wanted to talk. He was just trying to find a way to start. He had even been driving slower than usual— oh, he might pretend he was looking for deer or stray cattle or Gordon LaChapelle's car in the ditch—but she knew he was searching for words. He began to click his tongue the way he did when he was working up the courage to speak. And they had to talk in the car. When they got home, Wesley's father might be waiting.

Mr. Hayden was famous for his insomnia, and sometimes on nights when he couldn't sleep he would come over to their house and engage Wesley in endless games of gin rummy. If Mr. Hayden found Len McAuley awake and sober he'd bring Len along and the three of them would play pinochle. As long as those men were awake in her house, Gail couldn't sleep. She would lie in bed and listen to them at the kitchen table, the shuffle and slap of the cards, their strange counts—"Nine, twelve, thirteen, and twenty for gin;" "Rope for sixteen, aces for ten." Sometimes these were the only words they spoke. Since she didn't know how to play any of their card games, it seemed as though they were talking in code, some secret man language that they spoke to prevent her from understanding.

Gail could make things easier for her husband simply by starting a conversation. Anything would do, an observation about the stars in the spring sky, the way the baby stopped kicking when they were in the car. But Gail was determined to wait.

Finally Wesley found a way to translate those sighs and tongue clicks into actual words. "You didn't like that, did you?"

221

He expressed so exactly what she had been thinking that her heart suddenly flooded with feeling for him. She was tempted to call the discussion off. But only tempted.

"No, I didn't."

"Paul has good-paying customers. Men want to be able to bring their wives, their girlfriends out for the night. I want to bring you." This last remark was so unexpectedly tender that it too caught her by surprise.

"Why does it have to be that way?" she asked.

"What way?"

"So rough."

"I didn't arrest him. Is that what you think—I should have arrested him?"

"Not necessarily."

"What then?"

"It's not for me to say."

He went back to his silence and his tongue-clicking. He moved his hands back and forth on the steering wheel.

She relented and said, "Couldn't you have talked to him?"

"I talked to him."

"And?"

"And what?"

"What did he say?"

"He wasn't moving."

"So you moved him."

"I moved him. That's right."

She could feel his anger now, filling the car the way the scented night air would if she rolled down her window.

"Why didn't you wear your gun tonight?" She knew he

usually carried one on duty, but she also knew that he made an effort not to let her see it. Before he met her someplace or entered their home, he left it in the car or in his office. For all Gail knew, he had it under the seat right now.

"So I could shoot Gordon off his bar stool?"

"So you could—I don't know—make him move along without . . . without what happened." She hated coming to this point in an argument with Wesley. She had allowed him to get her off the path she wanted to be on—a lawyer's trick, she was sure.

Wesley was quick to say, "He's going to be all right. We made sure of that before we sent him on his way. Gordon's got a hard head." He seemed to say this in admiration.

Gail was ready to give up. He didn't even understand what was bothering her. He thought she was upset about what had happened to Gordon LaChapelle when at bottom she didn't care what happened to him, in spite of the impression she was willing to give. What she did care about—what she had discovered that very night—was the fact that her husband could sneak up behind a man and pull him off his bar stool.

From that night on she kept careful watch on her husband, wondering what other recesses of his nature had been hidden from her. She saw nothing. In every respect he was the quiet, gentle, thoughtful man she had married. During her pregnancy, he became even more solicitous, so much so it was difficult to believe that the same hands that nightly massaged her aching ankles and calves had grabbed a man by the hair. And that was only what she had *seen*—what else had he kept from her? She could not relax around her own husband, so convinced was she that this man would reveal something else that would make her wonder again who and what he was. But for all her careful observation she didn't see anything until the baby was born.

Wesley would not hold the baby.

In the hospital, Daisy McAuley, Enid Hayden, Carol Clifton—they all took turns holding the baby. But not Wesley.

When they brought David home, Wesley still showed no interest in picking him up. Oh, he would stand over the bassinet, beaming as if a light had gone on inside him, and gaze down at David. And when Gail held the baby, Wesley would crowd in close, moon-eyed with love for both of them.

Yet he would not take that baby in his arms. On one occasion Gail wrapped David snugly in his blankets—a package so tight and unmoving it could have come through the mail—and laid him on his father's lap. Wesley looked so panic-stricken that Gail immediately picked David up, mostly to relieve Wesley of his discomfort.

That was the reason Gail decided to return to North Dakota for a visit. To allow her parents to see their first grandchild, yes, but also to stop counting days, wondering if this was the one when Wesley would hold his son.

The wind rattled the window in its frame, and Gail reacted instinctively, huddling deeper under the blankets. When she was a child, that north wind meant the long walk to school would be even colder. She tried to think—when David started school, which route would he walk? Which street would offer him the most protection from the winter wind? Gail realized that she was moving in her mind though the streets of Bentrock, Montana. Of course, that was her son's home, his birthplace, where his father and his paternal grandparents lived.

Now that she thought of it, Wesley's father was the only man who had held David. When they brought the baby home from the hospital, Wesley's parents were waiting for them. They had brought gifts—baby clothes and a blanket and a rattle shaped like a dumbbell, and a new rocking chair with a cane seat ("for Gail when she has to get up for those 2:00 A.M. feedings").

Enid Hayden carefully folded the blanket away from David, exposing his red, wrinkled face. Julian Hayden practically grabbed David from Gail's arms. He lifted the baby high above his head. Gail was sure she saw David's eyes widen in alarm, and she thought she heard Wesley gasp. But neither of them said a word while Julian continued to hold their son aloft. "How does it feel to be home, boy?" Julian asked his grandson. "How does it feel to breathe this air?"

Gail had been in North Dakota for almost three days, and her own father had not yet held David. What was the matter with these men—did they think a baby was so fragile that it could be crushed or broken in their arms? Did they think their hands were unsuited for holding a child? That their hands were soiled with dirt and misdeeds and therefore unfit to touch the clean, the innocent? My God, what did they think human hands were for?

The wind gusted even harder, and Gail heard another familiar sound, like handfuls of sand being thrown against the glass. She knew what that meant: the wind had brought snow, fine-grained and icy, down from the north. This time Gail did not burrow deeper under the quilt. She threw the blankets off and went to the bassinet to make certain David hadn't wriggled loose from his blankets.

To her astonishment, the baby was already awake. He was struggling to lift his head as if he was desperate to see above and beyond the white wicker walls of his bassinet. His fingers clenched and unclenched, and his legs kicked determinedly as if they could find purchase in the thin cold morning air.

His mouth worked and contorted with the effort to suckle or cry or both, but for the moment Gail just watched him. As soon as he made a sound, as soon as he found a voice, she would pick him up. But not before.